THE HOSPITAL

Ahmed Bouanani

The Hospital

a tale in black and white

translated by Lara Vergnaud

with an introduction
by Anna Della Subin

A NEW DIRECTIONS
PAPERBOOK

Manufactured in the United States of America
New Directions Books are printed on acid-free paper
Originally published in French as *L'hôpital* in 1990
and reissued in 2012 by Éditions Verdier in Paris
and DK Editions in Casablanca
First published as New Directions Paperbook 1411 in 2018

Library of Congress Cataloging-in-Publication Data
Names: Bouanani, Ahmed author. | Vergnaud, Lara translator.
Title: The hospital : a tale in black and white / by Ahmed Bouanani ;
translated by Lara Vergnaud.
Other titles: Hôpital. English
Description: New York : New Directions Publishing, 2018. |
Includes bibliographical references and index.
Identifiers: LCCN 2018006021 (print) | LCCN 2018002150 (ebook) |
ISBN 9780811225779 (ebook) | ISBN 9780811225762 (alk. paper)
Subjects: LCSH: Tuberculosis–Patients–Fiction. | Hospital patients –
Morocco – Fiction. | GSAFD: Fantasy fiction | Psychological fiction
Classification: LCC PQ3989.2.B629 (print) |
LCC PQ3989.2.B629 H6713 2018 (ebook) | DDC 843/.914–dc23
LC record available at https://lccn.loc.gov/2018006021

2 4 6 8 10 9 7 5 3 1

New Directions Books are published for James Laughlin
by New Directions Publishing Corporation
80 Eighth Avenue, New York 10011

Contents

Introduction

FIVE HUNDRED ANGELS, each holding a bundle of fragrant basil, surround a single person as he is lowered into the grave, imagined the ninth-century eschatologist Ibn Abi al-Dunya. The basil is a restorative for the tiring exertion of exiting life. The angels attend to the body with perfumes and balms, but scatter when Munkar and Nakir arrive, fearsome fellow seraphs who have come to interrogate the dead. One must remember to sit up, the theologian warned; your finger will be the pen and your saliva the ink. If one replies satisfactorily to their questions, it is said that they will push back the walls of the tomb. The angels will dig a hole beneath you, exposing the fires of hell – just to show you a glimpse of what you escaped. They will create a window above you, opening up a view onto an exquisite garden, a landscape for contemplation and a cool breeze as you wait, with the rest of the cadaverous crowd, for the resurrection day. *The Hospital*, from its first sentence, takes place beyond death, and for that its author must answer.

A shaft of light descends through the ceiling and onto the kitchen table, illuminating from its center the mud-brick house where Ahmed Bouanani lived his final years. It catches the cobwebs and spills over a heap of pomegranates, too numerous for the bowl that contains them. A staircase leads to a terrace with a view over the steep hills of Aït Oumghar, a remote Berber village in the High Atlas. Through the winding dirt alleys, donkeys, sheep, and quiet children slink, past crumbling houses stamped with red handprints to keep danger away. In the distance, there are grape vines and olive trees without end and fields of gourds, fed by the abundant waterways of a spring. A gigantic nest crowns a whitewashed minaret: the work of a stork, impervious to the megaphones that call the village to pray.

It was here that Bouanani went into occultation in 2003, following the death of his youngest daughter Batoul after an accident in their home in Rabat. He left behind the city where he had lived for forty years, and with it, the archive of a life of unceasing creativity, which remained in his flat on the Rue d'Oujda, collecting dust. He left behind hundreds of reels of 35 and 16 mm films on the balcony that had once masqueraded as a dressing room; the costumes his wife Naïma Saoudi designed and dyed in the bathtub; the props and backdrops, impossible for an outsider to decipher their use. He left behind the thousands of books in his library; the boxes of illustrations and comics he sketched, the old photographs, film posters, and playbills. And he left behind the stacks of his manuscripts, written in black or blue ink in a steady, cursive hand and never published: dozens of novels and screenplays, hundreds of poems, short stories, journals, a history of Moroccan cinema, a chronicle of Morocco itself.

In the stillness of the house at Aït Oumghar there are ghosts of cats. In footage captured of Bouanani not long before his death in 2011, the cats – at least seven – swirl around his feet and jump onto his lap when he sits, wrapped in a blanket, to read. He is frail, hermit-like; there is an elegant nobility to his bearing, "like an emaciated Brahman," as a friend wrote, or like a certain prophet who would rather cut off his sleeve than disturb the feline sleeping upon it. Some called him "Sidi Ahmed," imbuing him with the title of a holy man. Those who once knew him and venerated him were discouraged from trying to find him in his mountainous retreat. Rumors circulated that he was dead, he was ill, "drunk from morning till night," bad-tempered, misanthropic, that it was impossible to pin his geographical coordinates on any map. Even in Aït Oumghar, Naïma's ancestral village, few knew that anyone lived in the house, for it was said Bouanani never went outside. His books – the very few that were published in his lifetime – were equally hard to locate. It was nearly impossible to find a copy of *L'Hôpital*, published in Rabat in 1990, *Les Persiennes* (1980), *Photogrammes* (1989), or *Territoires de l'instant* (2000), titles that were printed only because they had been pried from Bouanani's hands by friends and admirers. No images of the author circulated. In the rare event of a review in the press, it might be accompanied by a picture of the wrong Ahmed Bouanani – a television host with the same name.

On a cold day in 2014, I visited the house with Touda Bouanani, Ahmed's older daughter, a brilliantly imaginative filmmaker occasionally known to dress in drag as Fernando Pessoa. At the time, we were both artists-in-residence at Dar al-Ma'mûn in Marrakech, a few hours drive from Aït Oumghar. Touda strikingly resembles her father, in her features and her sage-like presence. As the last surviving member of her family, she is the self-appointed guardian of its memory. Through her, stories rise to the surface, a bit like Melville's Ishmael, afloat on the coffin and quoting Job: "*And I only am escaped alone to tell thee.*" I remember a portrait of her parents, drawn by Ahmed, watched over us in the kitchen. Naïma, who died in 2012, was depicted as twice Ahmed's size. She stared out at us and smiled; Ahmed was turned inwards, as if to bury himself in the folds of her scarf. He was writing on a pile of papers that rested against Naïma; his hair was a tangle of caterpillars. His eyes were looking down or were shut, against what he calls in *The Hospital,* in Lara Vergnaud's translation, "the world's angry and defeated face" – a face that he could never get used to. Ahmed Bouanani was an enigma, and he must have preferred it that way. But the inquisitive angels hate a mystery.

1. WHO ARE YOU?

In 1938 on the night I was born
this country had no more ancestors or History
It was a garbage dump where soldiers on the run
waded in grime and worshipped a deity
who, deaf-mute, twirled in the clouds
among locusts and naked angels

Ahmed Bouanani was born on November 16, 1938 in Casablanca, a colonized city on the verge of war. Through the shutters of his childhood home on the Rue de Monastir, he could observe his surroundings without being seen. What he saw was a world in the midst of modernization, haunted by the unavenged ghosts of a swiftly disappearing past. His was "the generation born of the marriage of the locust and the louse," as Bouanani would say, an unholy union between a species that nestles and one that invades from above. In 1912, Morocco's hamstrung Sultan 'Abd al-Hafid was forced to sign the Treaty of Fez, transforming the kingdom into a French "Protectorate," with limbs ceded to Spain. While the French decided to preserve the pageantry of the Moroccan palace, it was only a mirage of sovereignty, for true power now lay elsewhere. In modernist office buildings in the new capital of Rabat, a parallel government was erected to control the colony and subdue its insurrections. Within the vast bureaucracy, Bouanani's father worked as a police officer. In the hallucinations rising up from the narrator in bed 17, Wing C of *The Hospital*, the technocrats extend even into the afterlife. Certain angels direct traffic, others with desk jobs flip through folders, to "get acquainted with our infamies, rebellions, or submissions, and perhaps as well, some evidence, uncertain and unbelievable, of our humanity."

World War II brought swarms of American soldiers to Casablanca, along with air raids, famine, and chocolate bars. While Moroccans across the country rose up in scattered revolts against the colonial overlords, thousands of others fought and died alongside the Allies for a meager pay. A bomb fell on the house next door; Ahmed and his older brother M'hamed played at the war like a game. "Little Soldier Ahmed wears the shoes of a former combatant, he feasts with his eyes on Superman in front of the Cinéma Bahia where a police officer whips the crowd squabbling around the cash register," Bouanani recalls in *Les Persiennes*, or *The Shutters*, as translated by Emma Ramadan, a collection of poems in which childhood memories appear like butterflies pinned in a box. His grandmother Yamna, "the strangest being in the house," could still remember the French conquest, and taught her grandson that the souls of dead ancestors hide in the iridescent shells of beetles. Ahmed was sent to study with a Quranic teacher with a particular zest for doomsday. Gog and Magog lurched freely in the classroom as American zeppelins menaced overhead.

With the end of the war, the Moroccan nationalist movement stepped up its calls for independence, which were met with violent crackdowns and arrests. Although they demanded a democratic future for Morocco, the nationalists, to conjure support, drew upon the figurehead of the Sultan, Muhammad V, who occupied a nearly mystical stature in the popular imagination. In 1953, following massive demonstrations in Casablanca that were brutally suppressed, French authorities attempted to quell the national unrest by staging a coup and banishing the royal family to Madagascar – to the outrage of Moroccans across the country. It was said that the exiled sultan appeared in the moon; at night people climbed up to the rooftops for a closer look. Demanding Moroccan liberation and the sultan's return, roving militias attacked police officers and government bureaus. In the violence that ensued, thousands were killed.

The crowd on the sidewalk. Around a red circle. At eight in the morning. Eight fifteen in the morning. January of ... Someone had grabbed his 7.65mm revolver hidden in a pile of mint.... He fires the only bullet.... And the sun felt dizzy. Morning no longer knows which way to turn. The entire city, the walls, the lights, the new sky where the stars barely had time to turn on. Everything falls in front of my bicycle. Collapses. A police officer stops me. No, let him go, it's his dad. It's my dad. And the entire city says that it's my dad.

In early 1954, amid the wave of nationalist attacks on policemen, Ahmed's father was assassinated on the street not far from their home. Ahmed, who was sixteen at the time, did not witness the shooting but arrived soon after, and saw the stains of blood on the sidewalk. The killer was never arrested and his identity would never be known. "I began writing after my father died," Bouanani would recall in a journal entry. "Today I would say that writing was a refuge from my distress. But at the time, it was the legitimate ambition of an adolescent who wanted to get out of adolescence, who wrote, in his grand naiveté, also legitimate, on the first page of one of my middle school notebooks: 'I want to be Victor Hugo or nothing.'"

The following year on November 16 – Ahmed's seventeenth birthday – the Sultan, in his fez and sunglasses, stepped off a plane and onto Moroccan soil again, called back from exile by the French in a desperate attempt to restore order to a country in chaos. Greeted by enormous, rapturous crowds, Muhammad V announced the end of the Protectorate: a few months later, Morocco's Declaration of Independence would be signed. Ahmed, by all accounts a diligent student, finished his baccalaureate, and left Casablanca for Paris in the early 1960s to study film at the prestigious Institut des Hautes Études Cinématographiques. As soon as he received his degree, he returned to Morocco. It was 1963 and he was eager to contribute to the greater cause of a new, national art.

2. WHAT KNOWLEDGE DO YOU HAVE?

The screenplay? Come on! The actors are here. They're friends from bad neighborhoods. They're ready to throw themselves on Tarzan and tie him up to a tree trunk. That's all there is to it. From now on they'll all be available Saturdays and Sundays to transform into a strange painted tribe with feathers on their heads: a mix of Indians and savages from Africa and Central America. They don't really need costumes. Only the "bad guy" presents a problem: he's a colonist. He wears a hat, short-sleeve dress shirt, shorts, socks up to his knees, and polished black shoes. Oh yes, he's armed.

In the early 1940s, an illiterate paperboy saved up money to buy a 9.5mm camera, and filmed his own versions of Tarzan movies in the woods of Aïn Diab. The boy, Mohamed Osfour, tried to process the film himself, using household cleaners mixed with teaspoons of chicken blood – an act that Bouanani would hail in his unpublished manuscript *La Septième Porte* (The seventh gate) as the heroic and unlikely birth of Moroccan cinema. In 1897, the Lumière brothers immortalized a Moroccan goatherd; during the Protectorate, the country became a ready-made set for Orientalist fantasies on the silver screen, among them Luitz-Morat's *At the Entrance to the Harem,* for which the Pasha of Marrakech supplied 12,000 extras. Yet Osfour's homemade endeavors marked the first native film, Bouanani argued in the magisterial history of cinema he would write over the course of a decade.

In 1944, the Centre Cinématographique Marocain (CCM) was established in Rabat, a small office under the Ministry of Interior that served as the Protectorate's film regulatory institute. It produced short films to be screened in theaters before the feature, to extol the achievements of the colonial regime. In the mid-sixties, with the launch of national television, the Palace turned to the CCM to create films that would promote a sense of Moroccan identity. Upon his return from Paris, with few other prospects for employment, Bouanani took a job as film editor at the CCM, where he would remain for thirty-two years. He also took on work for government-sponsored heritage projects, to document Amazigh, or Berber, culture so rapidly disappearing. Sent on assignment to the remote Aït Bouguemmaz tribe, high in the Atlas mountains, Bouanani filmed them performing a circular, ritual dance. Yet when he inquired as to why they danced in this particular way, the chieftains replied that a French ethnographer called Jean Mazel had told them to, lending evidence to his theories on "solar dances." On assignment to document villagers in the town of Imilchil as they picturesquely toiled away at handicrafts, Bouanani was appalled to find soldiers supervising them with guns – and so he filmed them too. When he screened it for his bosses at the CCM, they berated their employee for "spoiling" the image of Morocco, and the film became Bouanani's first, of many, to be banned.

By the midsixties, the excitement of independence had given way to disillusionment, as the success of the nationalist resistance opened the gate for absolutism to reinstate itself in familiar forms. Following the death of his revered father, the cold-blooded Crown Prince Hassan II had risen to the throne. The regime grew ever more repressive, and traces of the colonizer still remained everywhere, from the language taught in schools to the thousands of French troops still stationed on Moroccan soil. In 1965, students rose up in protest in Casablanca, joined by the masses of unemployed and the impoverished dwellers of the expanding slums. Street battles between the people and security forces paralyzed the city, while the spirit of uprising spread across the kingdom. After several days, the riots were violently crushed by army tanks, as the king's military general hovered above Casablanca in a helicopter. With thousands killed, imprisoned, or disappeared, the slim Constitution suspended and Parliament dismissed, the brutal suppression marked the beginning of Morocco's *années de plomb,* or "years of lead." On national television, the king attacked the students who had provoked the revolt. "Allow me to tell you," Hassan II announced, "there is no greater danger to the state than the so-called intellectual; it would have been better for you to be illiterate."

For a generation stuck between locust and louse, the uprisings marked a political awakening. The following year, a group of artists and intellectuals established the radical journal *Souffles,* to which Bouanani contributed several poems and essays. In his manifesto, the editor and poet Abdellatif Laâbi railed against the stagnation of Moroccan thought and called for the total decolonization of culture and art. Yet what foundation was left upon which to build a national culture? What bound Moroccans together as a nation? After all, it was the colonizers, Laâbi wrote, who had come up with the boundaries of nations, artificial divisions that retraced the history of conquest and dismembered tribal zones. What made Morocco a unity beyond a shared history of defeat? Its conquerors had imposed an invented binary between "Berbers" and "Arabs," for the French had seized upon linguistic differences to pit two imagined "races" against one another. Often, colonial administrators extended special protections to the Berbers to alienate them from their Arab neighbors, in a classic tactic of divide and rule. "Are we really a people?" a patient called "Fartface" fumes in *The Hospital.* "Think about it. We were born with our right hands outstretched, begging in our blood, not to mention cowardice, infamy, and fear … We don't even know how to talk anymore, our people's pitiful vocabulary barely fits in the palm of my hand."

Under Hassan II, illiteracy was endemic, and in Bouanani's microcosmic ward, few of the inmates can read. When a villager in Wing A receives a rare letter from the outside (possibly non-existent) world, no one is able to decipher it except our narrator. Like a virus, illiteracy came in multiple strains: from aphasia to the peculiar wordlessness caused by a fall into the cracks between languages. In Moroccan schools, French contended with classical Arabic in curricula, which faced off with the tongues spoken at home: the colloquial Moroccan Arabic known as Darija; and several regional varieties of the Tamazight (or Berber) language. In the fray, the words for things – flora and fauna, tagine ingredients, musical instruments – were disappearing. In "The Illiterate Man," a poem published in *Souffles*, Bouanani wrote:

> *All the memories are open,*
> *but the wind has swept away the words,*
> *but the streams have swept away the words.*
> *We are left with*
>   *strange words*
> *a strange alphabet*
>   *that would be astonished to see a camel.*

In the wake of the humiliating defeat of Arab forces in 1967 by Israel, *Souffles* became more militantly politicized, and introduced an Arabic-language counterpart *Anfas*, with the aim of moving away from French. Yet for his own part, Bouanani began to distance himself from *Souffles* and continued to write predominately in French, the language of his education. He anticipated the criticism of writing in the colonizer's language, and took a characteristically cryptic, iconoclastic approach. "For me, all languages are foreign," he would say. "They resemble – pardon the metaphor – wild mustangs that need to be broken. I will let you imagine the rodeo." In an interview, Bouanani would recall how he once supposed cinema could be a universal tongue, an escape route from the politics of language – until he watched a Charlie Chaplin film with a crowd of Berber farmers, and no one laughed.

In the midsixties, with no other source of funding in sight, Bouanani learned how to use his government commissions to secretly, subversively, make the kind of films he desired. Assigned to document public infrastructure projects in the port of Tarfaya, on its ten-year anniversary of freedom from Spain, Bouanani created *Tarfaya, or The Poet's March* (1966). In the twenty-minute film, the history of the port city is narrated through a young man's journey across the desert to find a legendary poet-saint, a character inspired by the eighteenth century Shilha bard Sidi Hammou. On his mythopoetic quest, the protagonist encounters the craftsmen and construction sites that Bouanani had been sent to film. Bouanani would say that if the sequences fulfilling the instructions of his commission were edited out, the true film of *Tarfaya* would be unearthed: "It was not satisfying, but at least it was there, at a time when there were no other means of production," he told his filmmaker-friend Ali Essafi. Beneath the neutralizing surface of "heritage," the film masks a deeper anger. In a midnight scene, it appears a tribe's desert encampment is viciously attacked by a force we cannot see or grasp. But soon the viewer realizes it is only the camels – spooked by a howling, uncontroversial wind.

Deeply disturbed by the extinction of cultural memory he witnessed on his early assignments, Bouanani began a lifelong project to collect Moroccan oral poetry before it was forgotten. Few could remember the verses of Sidi Hammou, or the Tassaout poetess Mririda N'Aït Attik, or the many itinerant bands of singers, lute players, and tambourinists who once traversed the country, and who survived only as a tourist attraction in Marrakech's plaza Jamaa al-Fnaa. "Classical historians and biographers dismiss anything not composed in literary Arabic, casting into oblivion these 'vulgar and illiterate poets,' who nevertheless have expressed the deepest sentiments of our people," Bouanani wrote in a 1967 essay for *Souffles*. In the fight against colonial invasion, and during the Protectorate era, as tribes were driven from their land or forced to pay steep taxes, the troubadours were at the forefront of the resistance. Ever on the move between villages, disguised in fanciful costumes, they spread news of revolt in coded lyric. Bouanani quotes a poet from the Bni Mtir:

> I speak for those seated around me.
> If I said what I have to say to the spring, she would dry up with
>   rage.
> If I said it to the tree, he would lose all his leaves.
> If I said it to the rock, he would shake from side to side....
> All of you, you who have lived what my words report,
> Listen to me!
> You have eaten the meat of bitter fruit and your children's lips
>   are
> blistered!

The poets hoped that lines such as these would come to them in their dreams. They would visit the caves and tomb shrines of patron saints, to offer sacrifices and then fall asleep. If the sacrifice was well received, it was said the spirits would give the poet milk to drink and a plate of couscous. "The number of grains he eats will be the number of poems he composes," Bouanani noted.

In preserving folklore, Bouanani fought against the notion that it should be dismissed as superstition while another body of knowledge, European in origin, is elevated as history, science, philosophy, or art. Why should one be considered "mythic" and the other as "real"? And who should get to decide? Before history belonged to Europe, it was the property of Arabia, written with swords in the eighth-century invasion of the Maghreb, as Bouanani muses in the poem "My Country" – a parallel to that of modern-day imperialism. With the French conquest, and the rise of mass tourism, a new danger emerged, of tradition made counterfeit. As the poet Omar Berrada points out, Bouanani observed such simulacra in the Berber dances seeded by the French ethnographer Mazel. So too with the imposed fantasies of the *Arabian Nights*, which tend to appear in Bouanani's writings as infected, perfumed, and cheap; "stories in slippers with their falsely serene eyes." Moroccan artists must stop playing the "misunderstood little genie," Bouanani declared, yet the thighs of Scheherazade make their appearance myriad times in his fictions. Across his work, the folkloric is simultaneously degraded as an Orientalist invention and exalted for what it truly represents. "Legend is truer than history thanks to the amount of human information it provides," Bouanani writes. "The fictions it contains are neither grotesque nor childish: they express the true secret aspirations of a people, their spiritual quest for a world of wonder where human values triumph and where the laws they hate are abolished." It imagines a heaven where angels are susceptible to contagion.

Sometime in the autumn of 1967, Bouanani caught tuberculosis and ended up in the Moulay Youssef Hospital in Rabat. He wrote letters to his wife Naïma, who had just given birth to Touda the previous year. For six months, Ahmed stared up at the ceiling from the hospital bed.

This Saturday, December 9,

... Boredom has long, long legs and a cold, harsh head ... Even photographs are terrible to see. When will I return to their world? Maybe ... and maybe.

I wasn't able to write a single word Sunday, and it's even colder today. Earlier it was like the end of the world. In my cold little planet, I'm thinking of you. Warming my poor body beside yours, penetrating your blood in search of the sun. Thousands and thousands of times I hold you against my sick chest, I lose myself in your hair, in your eyes, and in your hips and in your stomach. My life stops and I have the entire universe in my head. My desire would endlessly fill the pages. One must shut up to hurt less.

Write me, tell me about your day, tell me about Touda's world. Take time to write to me.

The one who wants you,
you, always beautiful, always happy

Ahmed

"It's cold here too, like in my memory," the narrator writes in *The Hospital.* "No chance of nestling into the soft belly of an illusion." A swarm of insects flutter through his dreams, different species of butterflies "that my naked body attracted like a light." He is amazed he can still remember the names: "Urania, Vanessa, Bombyx, Argus, Machaon, and Phalene specimens." Armies of caterpillars creep along the contours of the night. When Bouanani was released from the hospital in May 1968, he received a certificate of good health authorizing him to return to work. The slip of paper, which Touda found years later, was signed by a certain Dr. Papillon, or Butterfly.

3. WHO IS YOUR LORD?

"Who was Caesar then?" Touda asks her father in footage captured in Aït Oumghar. "*Ghannam*," he replies. "And Hassan II." Not long before he was exiled to the TB ward, Bouanani suffered a banishment of a different sort. Although deeply political, the filmmaker preferred to float above party politics, and resisted any affiliations. Yet at the CCM, he was ever suspected of being a communist. When Omar Ghannam was appointed as its director, he deemed Bouanani a subversive element and ordered him to cut his long, flowing hair. Banned from directing any more films, Bouanani was relegated to the dusty archive department, and permitted only to work as editor. Yet surrounded by reels of moldering footage – documents of the French invasion and its "civilizing" mission – Bouanani soon realized that editing could be a way to overcome censorship and an art form of its own. He would resurrect the old newsreels, from the CCM collections and others he found on the site of a dismantled production studio, some of it so faded it appeared as ghostly white. Behind closed doors, like the spider of his hallucinations, he began weaving together archival footage into a clandestine, feature film *Mémoire 14*, which told the story of Morocco's subjugation and reflected upon its present day.

In the early 1970s, an increasingly autocratic King Hassan II led a movement to Arabize collective memory: to erase the deviation of colonialism from Morocco's history and eschew European curricula in schools. The record of national memory would begin only in 1956. To speak of anything earlier became taboo, and in particular any mention of a certain, ill-fated "Rif Republic." In 1921, the editor-turned-guerilla Abd el-Krim led a revolt to liberate the mountainous region of the Rif from Spanish and French rule. After a series of stunning, unlikely military victories, Abd el-Krim established the independent Republic of the Rif, which began to print its own banknotes, appointed a Prime Minister, and sought diplomatic relations abroad. After five years, European forces succeeded in violently suppressing the Rifians, using chemical weapons. Exiled to the Indian Ocean, Abd el-Krim became a hero of anti-colonial resistance everywhere, and the Rif Republic remained as a model of how the people might rise up together to create the kind of nation they wanted to live in. As its memory could not be spoken aloud, Moroccans would give folkloric names to the different years of the Rif War, as Bouanani captured in "Mémoire 14," a 1969 poem recited in the film that shares its name.

> *Years of the gazelle,*
> *years of the locusts,*
> *year of the sword and the canon,*
> *year of the fair season.*
> *Our blood still tastes like legend.*

The number fourteen conjures a conflicting way of measuring time, as the Islamic fourteenth century A.H. corresponds to the twentieth century C.E. – the designation ever prompting the question, common to whom? The dueling systems of time-keeping destabilize any authority time itself might have, that "invention of adults" which twists into absurd shapes in the eternity of a hospital ward. In the footage of *Mémoire 14,* reptilian army tanks scale a desert ridge; a man runs with a lamb in his arms as bullets fly; a plague of locusts descends upon the fields; the Sultan, swathed in white, appears beneath his parasol; a camel is shot in the head.

In 1971, Bouanani finished *Mémoire 14*, with a run-time of 108 minutes. Yet Ghannam found it inflammatory, and ordered him to redact vast sequences, especially the footage from the Rif War. With each new cut Bouanani screened, Ghannam demanded further censorship – and that the outtakes must also be burned. What was left of the film was a mere 24 minutes. "Our memory is long-lasting," the narrator declares almost mischievously. As Bouanani recalled to his friend Essafi, the tyrant Ghannam remained displeased by the film, threatened to fire him, and to see that *Mémoire 14* was destroyed. It was, fittingly, the intervention of history itself that rescued the film. Ghannam was invited to a birthday party for Hassan II in July of 1971, an extravagant feast held in the seaside palace at Skhirat. Just as lunch was served, a thousand mutinous soldiers stormed the banquet, overturning tables and raining bullets onto the guests. The King and his family escaped, yet nearly a hundred revelers were killed – Omar Ghannam among them. The first line of *Mémoire 14* repeats as its last: "Happy is he whose memory rests in peace."

In the wake of the failed, bloody coup, soon followed by a

second attempt, the response from the palace was immediate. Suspected plotters, traitorous generals, and large numbers of left-wing intellectuals alike were rounded up and forcibly vanished. They would be incarcerated in secret desert prisons that would only become known to the public in the 1990s, when the inmates who were still alive were released. Most infamous was Tazmamart, a remote sepulcher where hundreds of Moroccans were left for nearly two decades to die a slow death, confined underground in isolation, without light or basic medicine. Among the incarcerated was Naïma's brother Nourredine, a student at the time. After disappearing for two years, he was discovered languishing in Kenitra Prison; over the course of his ten-year imprisonment, Naïma and Touda were able to visit him. With him in Kenitra was Abdellatif Laâbi, whose 1972 arrest put an end to *Souffles-Anfas*. In a poem in their honor, Bouanani wrote:

> As soon as the guards turn their backs
> he flies
> he comes to greet us . . .
> The birds know you
> There are shreds of cloud in your beard
> wipe them off before going back to the walls
> Happy are my friends
> the poet prisoners
> for beneath the earth they see
> much further than us

"*Strange age*," a haunting voice announces in Arabic. "Hadn't our ancestors predicted this? Even dreams will be forbidden. . . . Forbidden . . . forbidden . . ." the voice growls. In 1979, after a succession of further tyrants at the CCM, a new, sympathetic director was appointed, Bouanani received a raise, and he was finally able to make what would become his only feature film – the cult classic *al-Sarab*, or *The Mirage*, based upon a screenplay he had revised for ten years. In the opening scene, two men haul sacks of flour along a hillside path, and argue over whether a donkey may be buried in a cemetery. Will a donkey be admitted into paradise? Their conversation evokes the Prophet's night journey to heaven aboard the winged steed Buraq, the ascent known as the *miraj* – a word so close in sound to *mirage* – from the Arabic root "to rise." One of the men, Mohamed, discovers bankrolls of dollars hidden in the flour. He sets out for the city with his wife Hachemia to exchange them for dirhams, in a quest reminiscent of *Arabian Nights* tales of men seeking their fortunes abroad. They encounter a ragged, raving messiah who captivates Hachemia. *"At the resurrection, everyone will have the same face,"* he preaches to his followers, who sit in a circle around him, chained by the neck. Meanwhile, Mohamed is too afraid to enter any bank, fearing its European keepers will assume he stole the money. When he meets a mysterious magician Ali Ben Ali, who claims he can help him, the naive Mohamed is drawn into a shadowy underworld of dissent, although its nature is never made explicit. Inside Ali's hideout is a gigantic canvas of Buraq – painted by Naïma.

Though the action is set in 1947, the film seems to juxtapose two eras: a Protectorate past and the unspeakable oppressions of the present years of lead. Mohamed discovers Ali lying in a dark passageway, gravely wounded, alongside other men, evocative of political prisoners. "May our powers of resistance equal our suffering," the magician declares as he slips unconscious. A Satanic child cackles at Mohamed, sending him into a panic. "I am just a poor man, I don't meddle with politics," he cries. When he escapes the tunnel, the world outside is in ruins; the grass has grown tall as if years have passed in minutes. He finds Hachemia deep in an ecstatic, communal trance, and drags her away. They reunite on the beach, in the warmth of an abandoned bonfire. A menacing group of drunken partygoers drives up to them in a convertible, wearing macabre masks, laughing in their faces. Mohamed's money was only an apparition; the poor will stay poor and must not even dream of becoming rich, concludes the sardonic fable of *The Mirage.* "My only ambition – and it's the ambition of all Moroccan filmmakers – is to get audiences used to seeing themselves and their own problems on the screen, and from that, to be able to judge themselves and the society in which they live," Bouanani would say in an interview. "The screen must cease to be the privileged mirror of foreign countries."

Bouanani had originally titled it "Some Dollars for Mohamed." When the title was rejected, he tried "No Dollars for Mohamed," but that too was censored, as disrespectful of the Prophet who shares his name. Mohamed appears again as a character in what would be Bouanani's most ambitious literary work, a monumental, never-published trilogy that he wrote over the course of thirty years. In *Le Voleur de Mémoires* (The thief of memories), a multi-generational family saga intersects with the national history of Morocco, in an epic it seems Bouanani never wanted to end. "I was happy to live with my characters," he recalled in a journal. Although certain friends knew he had been at work on the project for decades, it was not known until after his death whether it had survived and what stage of completion it had reached. "I don't like to end my novels ... It's like throwing these beings that had been my flesh, my blood, and my memory, into the arms of certain death," he wrote. "It's like closing a door on a paradise now lost and condemning oneself to stay behind, alone."

4. IN WHAT DIRECTION DO YOU PRAY?

No creature appears more frequently, across Bouanani's oeuvre, than the one with a horse's body, a woman's head, angel wings, and a mane as long as a cloud. Buraq is the winged embodiment of love, a symbol of the sacred that outstrips all religious authority. She transcends the dour theologians who despise her because her name appears nowhere in the Quran. In Bouanani's short story "The Resplendent Chronicle," a dissident scribe named Malek is wounded by an assassin's dagger, and is found in a pool of blood, still alive. On his deathbed, Malek gives his son the keys to the barn, where he housed a secret vehicle – the Buraq. His son Kacem unlocks the door to the stable, mounts the steed, and zooms off into the night. Centuries ago, when Buraq took flight with the Prophet Muhammad on her back, it is said she knocked over a jug of water with her hoof. When they returned to earth, having visited the seven levels of heaven and conversed with God Himself, the Prophet intercepted it before the water spilled out. Yet when Kacem descends from his own celestial journey, he finds, instead, that his father's house is aflame. "A gigantic blaze illuminated the sky. Everything around him was burning: the house, the books," Bouanani wrote, painting a scene that would prove eerily prescient. "The acrid odors of paper and flesh were wafting from the gutted ruins." For Kacem, everything is lost – his father's manuscripts, the relics of his childhood – except the Buraq, his inheritance, the creature that is his burden and his escape.

Late in the night on July 23, 2006, a neighbor in Rabat called Ahmed and Naïma to tell them that their apartment was on fire. It started on the balcony and first consumed the reels of films, the props and costumes, before spreading to the library, the boxes of manuscripts and photos, incinerating the bicycles, the television, and ultimately destroying half the flat. Its cause was never determined. "Sheets of paper fanned the flames," the police report concluded. What wasn't turned to ashes was drenched in the water that quelled the fire. Ahmed refused to return to the apartment, to witness the extent of the damage, or to ever estimate what was lost. It was Naïma who returned from Aït Oumghar to the heaps of charred rubble in Rabat and individually dried all the surviving papers in the sun. While the computers had melted, she found that many of Ahmed's hand-written manuscripts had miraculously survived unscathed, among them several wrinkled drafts of *The Hospital*. On the cover page of *The Thief of Memories*, water had begun to wash away the blue ink of the word "*Mémoires*" – but the text was still intact. Naïma found the slightly charred pages of *A Shroud for Naïma,* a novel Ahmed had written in 1971. She salvaged the waterlogged draft of *A Village Under the Sun*; so damaged that the pages, with their lines of perfect handwriting, had become translucent. She unearthed a scorched and molten Gallimard edition of Borges's *L'Aleph* that was still, somehow, legible.

A certain winged steed had also survived the flames. In the wreckage was the kitschy poster of an ornate, pink Buraq, decked out in jewels, with long black hair and heavy makeup – the model for the canvas Naïma painted for the set of *The*

Mirage. There was the drawing made by Ahmed of Buraq knocking over the jug. Spilling from it, in Bouanani's depiction, are sentences: words that flow into the blank and waiting pages of a nearby book. The picture itself had been soaked with water, and was laid out to dry in the warm July sun. There was a creepy image of a pink and green Satan stabbing Buraq in the heart. And there was Ahmed's drawing of Muhammad – he had drawn half the Prophet's face – astride the Buraq and amorously embracing her.

In Rabat, rumors circulated that Bouanani had died in the fire. Yet in the years that followed he was spotted at least once in the city he had forsaken – in a hotel elevator. Ali Essafi remembers bumping into him. "His body was like that of a ghost, but his spirit was lively, and his hand gestures elegant. His gaze remained youthful and piercing ..." Essafi was accompanied by a film festival director, and proceeded to make introductions. "My companion looked at Bouanani anxiously, and after fumbling for words, he asked: 'So you're alive?' Bouanani's answer was a mischievous smile."

Set in a place where no one is ever cured, *The Hospital* is a parable of resurrection. It unfolds within a labyrinth, a tomb that exists outside of time, whose inhabitants dress in "blue, two-piece shrouds." It is set within the enormous and failed infrastructure of an authoritarian state. Trapped in an unlivable present, the narrator will try an ascent, an abortive, feverish *miraj*, though he will not even scrape the bottom of heaven's outermost ring. "I glow bright as a star, I rise above the room to where I can barely hear my companions' breathing or snoring, I gently flatten myself against the cold ceiling, turn around so that I can look down upon the beds ..." he relates, before he flops back onto the medical cot. What *The Hospital* attempts is a resuscitation of memory: of a childhood pronounced dead and the collective memory of a kingdom forced to erase its past. "I admit to being a great amnesiac," the voice in bed 17 relates. "My memories resemble ruins eroded day after day." The inmates, like scrappy Scheherazades hooked up to IVs, tell each other well-worn tales to fight against the forgetting. In a place where memories become "bleach-flavored," their dialogue is full of vivid lists of nouns, as if taking inventory of a vanishing world.

The patients take pleasure in it: if nothing else remains for them, they can at least wrest back the words for things from oblivion. What emerges from their lists is a hospital that hardly – rather dysfunctionally – seems sterile at all. It has a fantastic garden. "All this vegetation around us! A caprice of a mad gardener ..." the narrator shouts. He begins to taxonomize. "Look around, we're not just talking oaks, pines, palms, or harmless poplars. There's also calabash, rubber, sumac, jackfruit, manchineel, sequoia, and baobab trees, and God knows what else! Not to mention the thousands of exotic flowers that have no business in a hospital." It is as if someone, an angel perhaps, has removed a wall of the tomb, offering a view onto paradise.

The Hospital attempts an excavation of memory, but it also poses the question: what's the point? What's the purpose of remembering, if at the resurrection, as Bouanani reminds us time and again, everyone will have the same face? Resurrection is the reawakening of the dead; the springing back into gear of joints and sinews unused for centuries as everybody gets up. But resurrection is also the resurgence of camaraderie, of communalism among the living, out of a crater of despair. The marginalized, impoverished, illiterate inmates of the hospital, abandoned by doctors and nurses, band together in unlikely friendships as they weather the freezing winds of a storm. They turn their meager meals into imaginary banquets; they mark occasions with grandiose speeches, like kings. They remind us, at every turn, of their humanity. Despite Bouanani's preoccupation with ancestors, *The Hospital* is not about what we owe the dead but about the barest minimum of what we owe the living. It reminds us that the afterlife is not only some shade of existence, postmortem, but also the collective living on – the continuing generations to follow our own. For their sake, it asks how to mend a country, when the rubble of white-washed memory is the only material at hand.

It was, by all accounts, a rather exciting moment to leave the planet behind. On February 6, 2011, the world was transfixed as it watched the uprisings of the Arab Spring. Only three weeks earlier, Tunisia's longtime dictator Ben Ali had been ousted by the protests ignited by a street vendor, who lit himself on fire. In Egypt, the Battle of the Camels had been fought in Tahrir Square, but Hosni Mubarak had not yet been toppled. In Morocco, protesters were just beginning to organize into what would form the February 20 Movement, later to be deftly contained by King Mohammed VI. Yet at this moment of political awakening and hope, Bouanani left the world, in the same, nonconformist way he'd lived in it. He died surrounded by his books in Aït Oumghar. When his death was announced, people mourned the wrong Bouanani – the TV host with the same name.

Ahmed Bouanani might have slipped entirely into oblivion, and been utterly unknown in English, were it not for the efforts of Touda Bouanani, Omar Berrada, and translators Lara Vergnaud and Emma Ramadan, chief agents of the auteur's resurrection in the present day. The poet, scholar, and curator Omar Berrada was reading old issues of *Souffles,* in an attempt to connect to a lost, earlier generation of Moroccan intellectuals, when he first stumbled upon Bouanani's name. He came across references to a mythical text called *L'Hôpital*, and visited every bookstore and library he could think of, in Morocco and in France, yet couldn't find a copy anywhere. Finally locating one on the internet in Uruguay, several years later Berrada was able to arrange for the republication of *L'Hôpital* in Morocco in the original and in Arabic translation, and an edition in France, in collaboration with editor David Ruffel. Berrada invited Touda Bouanani for an ongoing residency at the center he directs, Dar al-Ma'mûn, and has organized exhibitions, artist commissions, and talks in Bouanani's memory. Ali Essafi has created a Bouanani documentary, *Crossing the Seventh Gate.* The old apartment in Rabat has become a hive of activity – scanning, digitizing, collating pages fallen out of order, itemizing on color-coded spreadsheets – the physical labor of reanimating a writer from the grave.

Inspired by Pessoa's legendary trunk, Touda has transformed a painted chest from one of her father's film sets into a trove for his papers. In the esoteric *Les Quatre Sources* (1977), Bouanani's only experiment in color, which starred Naïma as a wild sorceress, the trunk concealed a sword passed down from a father to a son. Touda is only just beginning to reckon with the scope of her father's archive, and what to do with it. If Bouanani seemed to reject the idea of publishing, rather than face the censorship that plagued his films, the text themselves tell another story. Though written by hand, certain manuscripts are formatted as if they were published books, with lists of front matter – "Previously Published" and "Forthcoming" – detailing titles that Bouanani would never see printed in his lifetime. For his nonfiction works such as *The Seventh Gate,* his history of cinema in Morocco, Bouanani diligently prepared the indexes. Many of the drafts of novels, poems, and stories are illustrated with his drawings, of turbaned theologians, snoring peasants, mythic beasts. Among the papers is a copy of the first edition of *Les Persiennes*, which appeared in 1980 when Ahmed's daughter Batoul was eleven. She colored in the pages with bright magic markers, transforming the first page of her father's tome into a hybrid chicken-goat with claw legs. Later, in 1999, Bouanani would properly inscribe the copy to his daughter, four years before her sudden death: "For my Batoul, some lice and vowels from an earlier time. With an affection and a love that knows no limit –"

"Happy are those who can make of their suffering something universal," reads a scrap of paper from 1913, unearthed in Pessoa's chest. Over forty years of letters and moving pictures, Bouanani's elements remained remarkably consistent: a 7.65mm bullet, the sound of swallows, a cadaver, and a pickax, the view, half-light, half-shade, through the blinds. He leaves us with a corpus deeply evocative of his own Morocco, its particular species of lice, angels, and flies. Yet out of his strange alphabet, Bouanani has created a body of work that has withstood every torment of time. In the face of a world that remains angry and defeated as ever, Bouanani points us in the direction of the sacred. He passes along the keys to the winged steed to us. "I sometimes think I see that civilizations originate in the disclosure of some mystery, some secret," Norman O. Brown once wrote. "There comes a time – I believe we are in such a time – when civilization has to be renewed by the discovery of new mysteries ... by the undemocratic power which makes poets the unacknowledged legislators of mankind, the power which makes all things new." Ahmed Bouanani is such a mystery. Confounding archangels and autocrats, fire, water, and censorship, Bouanani comes to us, resurrected from the fragments of memory. With his Naïma, they are like the pair captured in an Amazigh love poem, which Ahmed put to paper before it was irrevocably lost:

A spring gushed up from the tomb of Fadel.
A spring gushed up from the tomb of Attoush.
They met each other and circled the world.

– ANNA DELLA SUBIN
NEW YORK, 2018

THE HOSPITAL

The only memory I have, after centuries spent living inside a
stone, is of the gentle touch of tears on a man's face.

– Michel Bernanos, *The Other Side of the Mountain*

WHEN I WALKED through the large iron gate of the hospital, I must have still been alive. At least that's what I believed
since I could smell the scents of a city on my skin, a city that
I would never see again.

As naturally as could be, I had fallen in behind one of
death's slow employees, I had added my name to a yellow
sheet already covered with flyspecks, I had said thank you four
or five times to heads nodding at me behind screens in tiny,
enclosed spaces where decades of paperwork and x-rays were
piling up on dusty shelves; and, as naturally as could be, I
hadn't bothered to turn around in the large hallway to salute
life one last time. I had abruptly found myself in another silence – later I'll call it the silence of a jar – on a planet inhab-
ited by caricatures of aging men, ghosts cloaked in coarse
linen, happy as trees or rocks, resigned even to their vomit.
The nurse leading me to Wing C proudly wore a Swiss watch
on his wrist, undoubtedly purchased on the black market. As
we walked, he'd announced the time twice to the groups of
invalids slumped on the ground or straddling the low walls. I
felt that perhaps this was his reason for being. Not only did
he shout out the time, but he also took care to specify the
seconds – and thousandths of seconds – to men frozen here
for days or weeks and who seemed to harbor all the necessary

indifference to the passage of time and changes in the calendar. Was it his way of distancing himself from this ailing humanity? To show them that he belonged to a realm of greater energy, vitality, and life?

I kept moving as if in a fog, at the end of which the men in white were waiting, I kept moving in a day that could not exist, telling myself: I am not afraid of hell, no, not the hell promised by the holy verses, but a hell without flames, without cannibalistic cooking pots, where they inject you, in small doses, with a slow death. Here, everything is foreseen, custom-built for us, it's normal that we are rewarded with a pitiful death, beneath tons of indifference and oblivion.

TO THOSE WATCHING, a drowned body rejected by the waves takes on the attributes of a monster – you turn away in disgust, or else observe at a distance, silent and respectful. Under the summer sun, the corpse is protected by anonymity. In horror, you imagine the multitude of creatures that fiercely tore into its skin and eyes, the small fish with sharp teeth who slid between still growing strands of hair.

The child whose name I once shared, now having taken charge of my sickly body, my face, my memory, resembles in every way this heaving form, stripped of all substance, which the ocean offers up to the astonishment of the living. To describe him I have only photographs in which he invariably adopts an awkward and timid pose. With such flimsy testimonies, it's hard not to smile, not to feel an emptiness in your gut. As for the impostor, he obsequiously drapes the corpse in a silk shroud. He rarely shows his true face. Instead his dates, places, and stories glisten like enamel, like the pure chrome of an engine.

My corpse doesn't bother me. I examine his festering wounds without self-pity. I can't resurrect him, I've forgotten too much. I suspect that, at the threshold of a poorly moored adolescence, my younger self destroyed his tiny world with a brutal kick in the teeth.

A labyrinth is waiting for me, full of dead-ends, blocked by the efforts of that damn wisp of straw whose corpse, out of time, taunts me with the smile of unshakable death. Here in this hospital, will I end up like the pilgrim dreaming of riches who, upon waking, shows me his penniless hands, minus a finger or thumb?

I admit to being a great amnesiac. My memories resemble ruins eroded day after day. The child that I used to be, within that distant edifice, has nearly erased all the faces, carefully rubbed away the events, the words, but he couldn't entirely destroy the memory of winters with tantalizingly frozen waters, or those of magnificent summers where the ocean beckons like a pleasure now forbidden to my fragile and sensitive body. Despite him, the homes of my childhood linger in smells that refuse to dissipate, in subtle noises, muffled until they're nothing but silences, infinite stretches of silence along which I struggle to put myself back together. And even when the miracle works, when a faint glow pierces the bedroom curtains and I see myself prostrate on a sheepskin stained with henna, miming one of the five daily prayers with a frightened fervor, my eyes blink, suddenly damp; the reflection of my image framed in a rectangular mirror with rounded edges then softens in the heat of the mirage. The child halts his prayer, lifts his head. Lines interrupt the serenity of his forehead. For a moment – an interlude of time that prolongs the flight of a fly – he searches himself, the taste of salt under his tongue. Something collapsed in the silence, with a motionless brutality. The child repeats the Quranic phrases in his head, turns them around in his mouth; the formulaic expressions take on the dull taste of things incomprehensible, opening up a void in which genuine hope, rid of the dross of legend, is nonetheless born. I rejoin my body just as the boy is being seized by wild joy. On the sheepskin, scarcely an eternity ago, the an-

cient wisdom of the stone filled me; now I break out in laughter that only I can hear; I stare at a ceiling that doesn't collapse
to punish me, and in the half-light of my childhood, for the
last time, I see God's grand stature crack, breaking without
majesty, scattering in fragments around my peals of laughter.

Stretched out in my bed, I'm looking at another ceiling:
between the two cement surfaces, time passed furiously,
draining my life like an anonymous, faded, and empty shell.

It's cold here too, like in my memory. No chance of nestling
into the soft belly of an illusion. The hospital is a frozen body,
walled in from every angle. Nothing survives here except
bones and men pale as lice.

I RUB SHOULDERS with death every day, that's why I no longer fear him. I see him in the eyes of my companions, dressed like them in squalid blue pajamas, smoking crappy tobacco like everyone else, shooting the shit while waiting for dusk. He doesn't hide in dark corners, behind parapets, under beds, in humid, stinking latrines – he joins us at the dinner table, he laughs along with us, he shares our madness, then he leads us to our beds the same way you'd try to tuck in a mischievous child who refuses to go to sleep. Is he waiting at the entrance to the wing, waiting for our eyes to close and our bodies to drift off in the dark? Only the dying truly recognize him when he materializes. He arrives at the restless sleeper's bedside, listening to his labored breath, inviting him to follow, without cruelty, without solemnity. One week after my admission to the hospital – I say one week even though I have only an approximate idea of time – death took a small old man from the neighboring room. He was the first to die during my stay, or more precisely, the first death in Wing C. Later I'll describe the hospital. For now, it seems immense to me – perhaps it had been imagined and built without any plan at all in the middle of a forest in the city suburbs. The number of wings itself is unclear. To find out, I'd need to go on more walks, to push a little farther each day; but, since my arrival, as I wait for someone to prescribe a specific treatment, I've stayed in bed practically every day and every night. I only leave the room long enough to stretch my legs and quickly eat my meals on the veranda.

I rose to go see my first death.

When the old man's passing was announced, his roommates immediately set to robbing him, scrambling after his meager loot: his threadbare babouches, a few intact mandarins, and a barely touched chocolate bar. "Hey now, cocksucker!" The guy yelling this is tall; he straightens up, and there's a free-for-all to divide the spoils and avenge slights in a manly brawl. "Damn Satan! come on you Muslims, damn Satan!" A Quranic schoolteacher intervenes, but the Muslims don't have time to damn anything, since now two other imbeciles have come to blows over a pack of Casa Sports discovered under the pillow. Meanwhile, I'm amazed to see a teenager leaning over the corpse and playing with its lifeless penis. Finally, two orderlies show up. "So the old man croaked?" While one of them pulls the dirty sheet over the dead man's face without bothering to close his eyes, the other, God bless him, sinks his teeth into the stolen chocolate bar.

I returned to the bed that I regretted leaving. I closed my eyelids tightly in the absurd hope of erasing the cruel reality of my surroundings. You're going to have to get used to it, I tell myself. After all, death is banal – didn't you once write that it's custom-made for us, hopeless as can be? If you shit a brick every time one of us sputters out like a fart, it'll kill you for sure. And anyway, honestly, you never paid any attention to the old man's existence, you don't even remember seeing him alive, so who cares? Isn't he lucky to die at his age? Get it together, for fuck's sake, and follow me. Stand in the hallway, listen to the gurney squeak by, and voilà – an empty bed for another candidate. Come closer, touch the spot where the old man used to lie, you can still see it; the dead don't give off any heat, there's nothing left but a smell they'll be hurrying to get rid of soon enough. And look, here they are, back already. Whenever the removal of a corpse is involved, the nurses turn into magicians. Step aside, they're going to move the mattress out into the sun. Now the little guy is definitively gone. Come on, let's light a cigarette, take a deep breath, avoid looking at the mattress, and laugh hysterically for no reason.

The corpse stayed at the morgue for several days. I can no longer remember if anyone came to claim it. When I questioned the kid from Salé, the one who was fiddling with the dead man's penis, he burst out laughing and started talking about the wild animals at the zoo in Temara. Then, in a serious tone: "In three months he only ever received one visitor, an old peasant woman from the South. His mother or his wife. They camped out under that tree, over there, to drink some tea. I haven't seen her since. But the old man got into the habit of drinking tea every Friday at the base of the tree."

What sorrow.

What sorrow over there at the base of that tree. If only I could find myself at its very top, touching a horizon, a bird, a cloud, inhaling down to my lungs the sweet smoke of a eucalyptus fire rising and rising in the blissful silence of the countryside! Well fuck it. Do I need my recollections, my bleach-flavored memories to ensure that I survive like the tranquil lizard? Perhaps I should imitate the other patients instead and listen to tedious and mind-numbing songs on the transistor radio, engulf myself in this insignificant present where graves eagerly await us, surrender myself to the hands of a merciful marabout – why not? – claw at my cheeks until they bleed, wallow in the ashes like a mule. Why do I need the memories of rotting, human wrecks, the shambles of the year of my birth, a 1938 populated by the damned, the plague-stricken, the paralyzed minds of the starved and sex-crazed? Fuck it. Through the stars and clouds and silences, here I am, once again a prisoner of my childhood street, the Rue de Monastir where rag sellers rubbed elbows with lepers. Who'll toast a glass of red wine or spirits to the phantom zeppelins that once passed through the low sky, triggering the warning sirens of a war whose children chalked hopscotch squares or swastikas like cabalistic signs on the sidewalks and walls? Our heroes were broad-shouldered behemoths with slangy nick-names out of *Faubourgian* novels that weren't worth a wooden nickel, facing off between two memorable benders before rushing into a colonial brothel and into dreams where their clammy gazes would confuse angels for whores with ten thousand franc bills pasted to their foreheads – the angels having escaped from a cruel paradise and the second-rate whores wearing rags that badly hid poor, aching bodies kneaded by generations of legionnaires, drunk sailors, starving Bedouins, and teenage explorers sneaking out of movie theaters and purgatory-mosques. One by one, then in bunches, the madmen float up to the surface of my forgetting, wearing *djellabas*, jeans, rags, or else shirtless, biceps and chests thrust forward, puffed out like sugarloaves, posing for a fleeting eternity before the lens of a street photographer. And what marvelous men of legend glisten in their eyes, bright as undying fireflies! Glory to the god of the vagabonds and their concubines with pubis crowned in cloves, I applaud you, inhabitants of new adventures and city jails alike, I applaud you, princes of nights that no one will ever write about, let's shake hands, let's have a seat here between these disemboweled trash cans, let's imagine an impossible dialogue above the gutters draining through gleaming sludge the skies that once were, when everything was in harmony, unless you'd simply rather puke out your cold insides? As for me, I'll keep you company, no hard feelings.

My dreams are over, brutally drawn to a close, they've retreated just below the surface like beaten dogs, my cruel golden dreams where I thought I would remain alone until the day I died. But I haven't left the present. Like a drunken Buddha I struggle to emerge from the spindrift of dust, I ask myself who these hands belong to, what fever is feeding me. The night weighs heavy like a donkey's body mangled by my claws and teeth. The trees, the sea, the town, a crystal ghetto, or the desert, yes, a desert is watching us, you and me, and all the others; a desert where, almost like laying a trap, they constructed this hospital stinking of trash and vomit and a sharp pharmaceutical odor. I tell myself like a refrain: they built this hospital to heal you, pal, heal you of your rotten ways of living, of blathering without end about death and an ill-digested and ill-fated life, here where the old man will die a thousand, thousand deaths . . .

EXCEPT FOR A student in his second year of medical school, who's had bad luck with microbes, all my cohorts are illiterate. Their collective library contains fragments from the Quran, shabby scraps from *The Perfumed Garden*, *A Thousand and One Nights* seasoned à la Marrakesh, and Juha's trickster stories. They're porters, stevedores, storekeepers, the unemployed, smugglers of every kind, the rejects of inexplicable wars and an aborted nationalist resistance, farm boys without land or bread, left behind by chance like febrile, rerouted castaways with a cargo of off-seasons and coarse language, still smelling of cornbread and cow dung; sickness has transformed them into wobbling, spitting diurnal specters, always a spirited insult on their tongues.

"They're a bunch of poor bastards," the kid from Salé says (later I'll start calling him Rover). "But be careful, there's some real pigs too. You see that guy over there scratching his belly button, he looks like an Arabic schoolteacher straight out of a dusty novel by Al-Manfaluti, and yet he's capable of selling his mom and dad for 'a fart in a windstorm'! The other one, sitting on the bench, owns a food stand. At night he used to hunt the cats of Salé with his two kids, both expelled from university, and his customers were always happy to eat rabbit for cheap! And look at that walking skeleton, between the trees, he's looking for a quiet spot to smoke his hash in secret. They say that he found his wife in the arms of the barber – and

47

you know what he did? No, of course not, you'll never guess. He was holding an axe and he forced them to keep going, honestly, he threatened to chop them up into little pieces if they didn't cum! You can imagine it, right? In a similar situation, I wouldn't have been capable of getting it up!"

I look at this babbling fetus and ask him his age. He smiles.

"You're right. Sometimes I'll say anything, it must be the medicines that are screwing up my head ... unless it's congenital!"

He smiles again and continues. "When I was born no one bothered to write down the day and time in any kind of registry. I think that an unknown mother had me clandestinely, that a benevolent father raised me clandestinely, and that today it's my turn to live clandestinely. Yesterday, I thought maybe I'd reached puberty ..."

"While fiddling with the old man's prick?"

"I thought that he wasn't circumcised ..."

"And?"

He looked at me like a surprised dog cowering to avoid being struck.

This is where I let myself be swept away by anger and contempt. I'm not safe from contagion. Without a doubt, without even noticing, I'm shaky on my feet too, I'm pitching like a drunken boat, pupils yellow, facial features crazed. I tell myself: it's no accident that the hospital administration didn't put mirrors in the washrooms. And for that matter, what would be the point of dolling yourself up every morning in this walled-in universe?

I didn't leave my bed this morning. While the bottle of serum emptied drop by drop into my veins, instead of gazing at the ceiling – and imagining living, elusive figures in the stains that bear witness to past winters, or taking an interest in the carousel of flies whirling without end around the naked light bulb that's shut off inexorably every night at nine o'clock, plunging us into a semi-darkness that illuminates sorrowful landscapes along which my body drifts in search of a merciful memory that will protect me from dissolution – I reread these pages without recognizing my handwriting, and then understand that my hope of remaining intact was like that of a drop of salt in the ocean. The air in this place facilitates the growth of bizarre fungi in the imagination. At all hours I am caught between vertigo and delirium. Every day I feel my memory heal over its scabs; I am reduced to a skeletal being, unappetizing even to the crows and vultures that I sense circling around me in my nightmares. I'm going to have to get used to living with my companions of misfortune in this world no stranger than any other, where, on occasion, despite my best efforts, the silence resuscitates painful seasons. And my companions? Mostly they no longer have any reason to leave, lost as they are in the density of their dreams. Whereas, I feel as if I came here for the day, two weeks, or a century ago, and forgot to leave. Where would I go? To another time, beyond the hospital walls, somewhere that I had a name, an occupation, a reason to exist. Today, my name is a number, I occupy bed 17 in Wing C, I am a rumpled blue pajama among other rumpled blue pajamas, a member of a melancholic and joyful brotherhood that hasn't asked any questions for a long time. I'm not confessing, and I don't claim to describe things that I know nothing about. I'm not trying to relieve my conscience the way you relieve your bowels or your bladder, I don't flatter myself, for the most part I don't pretend that my shit doesn't stink, so, if you're waiting for me to start whining, to spin infantile flights of fancy about my people and our dark ages, then hurry up and pawn me off on to your usual middleman and let's be done with it.

THE NIGHT – the first or the thousandth – after the death of the old man, whom I imagine spread out on a morgue slab, illuminated by a spectral light, I beat at my visions with savage blows, jeering, walking, stumbling, floundering, and sinking into the marshes up to my waist, harassed by cormorants, bloodied seagulls, bats, rains, tempests of cries, howls far too human or not human enough. Exhausted, I stopped myself and thought aloud: I really need to shut up my brain, I need to build a dike around my body if I don't want a humanity steeped in shit and lies to overrun my walls. Then: What am I talking about? You can't tell a nightmare what to do, and this is an exceptional one. It grabs me by the throat and hurls me into a garishly painted future full of cathedrals or maybe railway stations that trap trains and red-hot steam engines along with thousands of panicked travelers who are no longer going anywhere. All of a sudden we're alone – the old man and I – and our stage is moving, its outlines undetectable. The old man rises, his penis stiff as a billy club, he slides on his babouches and tells me in his childlike voice: "Come on friend, we're late, can't you hear the archangels' trumpets?" And my legs drag me into a monstrous resurrection. One-two, one-two, one-two! They arrive in legions, draped in rotting shrouds, foreheads branded with red iron by winged mercenaries, in a crush of bones barely sticking together, painfully staying on their feet, searching in their empty skulls for memories of a terrestrial existence with the despair of a horde of old men devoured by lice. The angels direct traffic, organizing the crowd, some brutally whipping along the professional mourners and the gossips, others, whose function I don't understand, colliding with the latecomers, impaling vaginas or cruelly biting scraps of breasts and buttocks. Fearing a similar fate, the old man, with me right behind him, runs for it with the agility of a guy in the prime of life. "This way, ladies and gentlemen of the free resurrection. Let's take a look at your records!" A tall, bearded brute with a white toga is yelling at the top of his lungs. He licks his thumb and index finger, slowly, to flip through folders stacked across miles of sky until the next eternity, to get acquainted with our infamies, rebellions, or submissions, and perhaps as well, some evidence, uncertain and unbelievable, of our humanity. How long did I wander in a panic, pursued by howls and death rattles, the cracking of vertebrae, the plop-plop of brains marinating in the celestial muck? There I was among odd characters who railed against their guardians; then among grandiose and arrogant men and women loudly insisting on a proper resurrection, refusing to appear in such lowly company, and demanding shrouds of pure silk, jewelry, chasubles worthy of their ranks, and other privileges. The old man had melted into a crowd where everyone had the same face: it was pointless to look for him and also impossible for anyone to recognize me, since I too – mine was an internal pain – had the same face as the others. Hallucinations rained down on me like a thunderstorm. I thought I saw members of my family, ancestors from our genealogical tree, long dead friends. Someone (was it my father?) stopped me and said, "In a few minutes, we'll both be the same age. Funny, isn't it?" Then, an old friend who'd hanged himself in a shitty hotel room put his emaciated hand on my shoulder – I identified him thanks to the towel knotted around his cervical vertebrae, which still displayed the hotel's initials and logo. He was crying but no tears came out. How long did I wander in panic? You have to be careful in eternity. When leaving Earth with the Messenger of Light in the saddle, Al-Buraq, the beautiful monster with the head of a Hindu woman and eyelashes heavily painted with kohl, inadvertently knocked over a jar full of water. The legend says that once back on Earth, after multiple peregrinations through the seven heavens and a long conversation with an enormous tur-ban-shaped cloud, the Messenger was able to stop the fall of the water jar so that not one drop was lost. (Which goes to show how precious water is in Arabia!) When I, in my turn, landed in Wing C, I had no jar. My skin stunk of the resurrec-tion, a foul mix of sweat, fenugreek, and suppositories. As I was cleaning under my bed, I discovered several tibias and shoulder blades garnished in sections by flaps of flesh that would have pleased a senile cannibal; I understood that the nightmare was persisting, tenacious as leprosy. It's possible that the old man was cut up into pieces much to the delight of the cannibals, it's possible that this crowd has been swarm-ing in invisible realms for thousands of years. I repeat this to myself so that the nightmare continues, so I don't feel the small bite of the IV, so I don't hear the "in the name of God, in the name of God" of the nurse in his fifties whose gurney squeaks through the hallway every morning at 8 a.m., so I can escape the other litany coming from my neighbor bellowing excerpts from the Quran at the top of his lungs. I close my eyes, still unaware that the barrier between my dreams and reality has grown too thin. I call with all my strength on merciful visions: Please God, transport me to a spring, a flowery orchard, the base of a fig tree, the edge of the ocean! Transport me to where my nostrils are intoxicated with the scents of the earth, where my ears hear nothing but the robin's song. Goddammit! I hear a rasping voice, I try to isolate it among the noise in the room – but there's nothing to be done, cries and laughter burst out like insults against disease, all disease, against the minions of medicine, against the unpredictable Minister of Health. Then, again, the rasping voice, more audible: "Look here, esteemed surgeons, I'm making you a gift of my spleen, my cavernous lungs, my testicles – one pound of good meat! – my intestines, my liver, which, granted, is nothing but a poorly patched-up scrap-heap, but what can I do about it? When you're born a dockworker, a pickpocket, or a rag merchant, you can't afford to pay for spare parts! But make no doubt about it, on the Day of the Reckoning we will be resurrected in brand-new bodies!"

ANOTHER DAY WITHOUT note, monotonous and flat, when we amuse ourselves by seeing who can spit the farthest, not me (I got conned into a tracheal tube), but the others, the young ones, accustomed to yelling in unison, flies open, fists at their hips, who pride themselves on running sprints without losing their breaths. I see them on a shaded path, cawing like crows. The gang's leader is unbeatable at spitting. We call him "Guzzler." Barely seventeen years old, he got used to leading at an early age, to throwing his weight around, no doubt because, born of a deeper or more insidious poverty, he instinctively understood that in a world of violence, "things" like kindness and generosity were a waste of time, and signs of weakness to be hidden like a shameful disease. Guzzler used to trawl the western side of town, near the ocean, where city officials had the second-rate solution of constructing a long and sinister wall to act as a folding screen to hide the endless rows of shantytowns from tourists. The children of those *douars* meet up near the rocks at dusk, to chug plastic bottles of red wine or, failing that, wood alcohol mixed with lemon soda. Fleeing the overcrowded slums, they consider this no man's land to be their true home, and any unfortunate couple that ventures there in search of a sunset should be forewarned. This is the kind of anecdote Guzzler loves – he tells them with glee. Two or three days before he threw up no less than a liter of bad blood, he and his friends had a good laugh at the expense of two young newlyweds driving around, looking for somewhere to make out in the seaside breeze. Guzzler starts to giggle like a schoolgirl.

"Oh man did we have a good time! Think about it, a barely healed vagina perfumed with Lancôme for God's sake – and that's not even the half of it! The husband was shaking all over, he was begging, groveling on his hands and knees. 'Take my wallet,' he moaned, 'take all my money, I'll give it to you, and here, take my bracelet chain and my watch, they're both solid silver! But don't touch my wife, please!' Idiot! Worthless pimp! He thought we only wanted at his bitch. Here, in this neighborhood, we don't quibble over details. A hole's a hole! So while a few of the guys were tearing off his pants, me and the others were fucking his unconscious wife. It felt like penetrating a fresh cadaver, a warm, quivering cadaver like a doll in a store window, and believe me, there's a lot more pleasure to be had, way more, in manipulating an inert and limp body just as you please – you take advantage of all the holes without having to ask permission. By the end I was going at it so hard my knees were covered in blood ..."

The gang laughed. Hyenas. I stayed alone on the path. Guzzler and his followers disappeared. I found them later on in the bathroom, they were masturbating their hearts out, no doubt imagining the unconscious woman.

A little before dinner, which was always served at 5:00 p.m., I smoked a cigarette with Rover. By way of preamble, he loudly blew his nose before telling me not to pay any attention to Guzzler's stupid boasting.

"Every year he tells the same story with one or two extra details. Who the hell ever told him about Lancôme perfume?!"

"He comes back to the hospital every year?"

"Like everyone, like all of us. Hmm, every year, every three months, what's the difference? In a way, the hospital has become our home. Once you're healed, you'll leave, but us? Come on. Where will we go?"

He pauses to take a puff on his cigarette, spits out a bit of tobacco, and asks: "You're not mad at me anymore?"

"Huh? Why?"

"But I don't see what the harm is. Once you're dead, a penis isn't good for anything, even less so when it belongs to a septuagenarian who hasn't gotten a hard-on since the Protectorate!"

Before I can figure out that he's alluding to the dead old man, he moves on: "I had a grandfather who looked like him. He wasn't really my grandfather – I called him that to make him happy but also out of habit. People would respectfully call him 'Al-Haj' even though he never set foot in the Kaaba. His memories stretched all the way back to the end of the last century, and he would soliloquize about the reign of Sultan Moulay Hassan I as confidently as he did about the conquest of the moon."

Rover speaks with a verbose eloquence that I find more and more surprising. The words tumble out of his mouth so fast that it would have been hard for anyone to interrupt. He fills the silence to avoid feeling the passage of time. Aside from another sleeping patient, we're alone in the room; the others are outside, taking advantage of the sun. I'm in my bed, Rover is at my side like a visitor come to notify me that time no longer exists, evoking the memory of someone from another era: the owner of a Moorish bathhouse who used to sponsor various businesses, marriages, circumcisions, divorces, and reconciliations, nothing happened or didn't happen without his presence, without his permission. He sat on his throne in the changing room of his bathhouse, which transformed by turn into a dating or real estate agency, neighborhood courtroom, charity, and forum for varied debates.

Rover relights his extinguished cigarette. I hear myself ask if the Al-Haj of the bathhouse is still alive.

"He's the kind of man who doesn't die easily," responds Rover. "He's probably still alive, if being shut up in a mental asylum can be considered living. Do you think that it's possible to lose it, just like that, from one day to the next, to have your brain functions fall apart like a car whose spark plugs, cylinder head gasket, and radiator all give way with no warning?"

Rover, once again, stops talking. He stares at the ground, transfixed. You could say that a spring, stretched as far as it can go, had snapped. Later, I'll understand that the medications provoke not only this secondary state between vertigo and nausea, but also his memory lapses. Rover continues his story, as if there'd been no interruption. He tells me for the second time that Al-Haj was the owner of a Moorish bathhouse, that's why he knew everyone and everything – even the most insignificant events. Seated on a prayer rug in the changing room where his clients liked to linger and gossip, Al-Haj looked exactly like a Baghdad caliph in the middle of his harem, the air laden with hints of sweat, armpits, and scrubbed flesh, rather than with perfumes of the Orient. As soon as he started speaking, everyone shut up. His voice reverberated. When he chose to ignore his clientele, he would take a pipe out of a small box and carefully stuff it with hashish. He then surrounded himself with an opaque cloud, and no one dared disturb him. Some suspected him of being involved in smuggling, some even accused him of owning hashish plantations in the North, in Ketama and Targuist ... "At the same time, anything is possible," Rover adds with a smile. "Our neighborhood barber is a police snitch, honest to God! Hoummane, the taxi driver, is in reality an inspector for the general intelligence services, so yeah, they say the old man was knee-deep in questionable dealings, but what could be more normal in a rotten world where we're all so suspicious that one day we'll end up betraying our own children?"

WHETHER WE'RE HUNGRY or not, the last meal of the day is hastily served at 5 p.m., one hour before the nurses leave. The patients in each wing set the large tables themselves, in a clamor of chairs being unceremoniously moved onto the veranda tiles. Rover flicks away his cigarette butt and tells me we should go eat. He adds as he rises: "The first are always the best served." I'd barely gotten out of bed and he was already gone. Nothing in the world could have turned him away from the table, he was always among the first to volunteer and after checking the menu he would help hand out plates, forks, knives, and glasses. In the beginning, he used to tell me: "Follow my lead, I manage to convince myself that I haven't eaten since the day I was born! It's close to the truth, I've gone hungry for so long that that my stomach has gotten used to digesting just about anything." On other days, with minor variations, he would say: "I know people who have eaten shit – for real – and they didn't die from it, so you shouldn't turn your nose up my friend, you aren't at your house or your parents' house anymore, and if you don't want to die with your mouth open, eat! So come on, let's eat some shit, and then some more shit – after all, even the most sumptuous, the most refined, the most delicate food ends up as shit, right?" Little by little, after defeating the knot in my stomach that was preventing me from swallowing anything at all, I had acquired almost robotic reflexes. I would stuff the food down blindly, thinking about other things – a distant wedding, dream-like tagines – anything that had the power to yank me out of my chair and transport me far, far away from the foul banquet. In truth, it was fear that overcame my reluctance. "It's the beginning of the end" is what they always said when a patient could no longer leave his bed. I would see the frightening pity in my companions' eyes, deference for someone already possessed by death, who will waste little time in showing that his place is no longer among the living. Yet that day, I didn't have to rely on my imagination. I was thinking about Rover's story. I was among the small group gathered near the doors to the Moorish baths. It was dawn, the mist hadn't yet dissipated, the first birds were bursting into morning song. Everyone's patience gradually gave way to exasperation, then concern, because Al-Haj was always the first to wake in Salé. "The rest of us, to make the time pass," Rover said, "told ourselves that the old patriarch barely had time to go from one warm body to another – and there were three of them! – before the voice of the jealous *muezzin* would remind him of his Muslim duties." Nothing in this neighborhood went unnoticed. Soon curious passersby, neighbors, and gawkers with their habitual purchases of beignets and tufts of fresh mint joined the small group of people who had come to take their weekly bath or purify themselves after a night of matrimonial lovemaking. A tall, muscular guy, moving away from the crowd, began to call toward the closed windows on the second floor – the old man and his family lived above the baths – but his powerful voice had no effect. "We should call the police!" someone suggested. "Since when do the police take care of us?" came the terse retort. The door to the house wasn't locked. A young baker, accustomed to entering everyone's homes, walked upstairs. He reappeared a minute later, looking confused, and told the crowd that there was nobody on the upper floor. "It's empty, as if the tenants had moved out during the night," explained Rover. "But, in Salé, nobody can move out without the whole town knowing about it, especially when it's not just any old family! Once alerted, the police turned up immediately and didn't waste any time – they smashed open the heavy door to the Moorish bathhouse …" This was the part of the story where Rover had stopped and disappeared. He had already greedily started into his ration of rice and fish when I sat down next to him. Guzzler and his gang were making an infernal racket, drumming on their plates with knives and forks. The same scene – or nearly – played out every day with the Machiavellian goal of stopping the "timid souls" from eating in order to hog their rations. Guzzler would impose silence around him, declining the honor of making a special speech ("Not today, fellows, inspiration has left the building through the toilets, it went down the drain with a ton of wormy diarrhea mixed with a couple pounds of solid suppositories ill-digested by our poor intestines") and propose – for a change – a riddle. ("The happy winner will enjoy a free special dessert composed of a scoop of seasonal fruit and fresh cream seasoned with yellowing pus, turds, gangrenous bedsores, expectorations, and frothy syphilitic sperm!") It goes without saying that, in the beginning, my appetite, seriously tested, would leave me at a gallop. And Rover, between two mouthfuls: "Make do with a glass of water, good idea, and when you're reduced to a corpse-like state, it will be our pleasure to bring you to the morgue accompanied by flutes and tambourines!" All that was in a distant past, when another version of myself would watch as his pride was washed away every day, another version of myself completely foreign to the man who, chewing on cold fish and rice, now managed to maintain the same rhythm as Rover while Guzzler loudly asked: "Do you know why the Slaouis lose their minds after four o'clock in the afternoon?"

Bursts of laughter everywhere.

"Well, I'll tell you."

The owner of the food stand interrupted, the one who hunted cats, and since he hardly ever talked during meals, his voice shut the whole room up: "Well, we don't give a fuck!"

"Who doesn't give a fuck?" Guzzler stuck out his chest, but his confidence had already been whittled down.

"Me to start with. And I'm laughing my ass off ahead of time because I eat losers like you by for breakfast. By the dozen. Furthermore, wise guy, I'll ask you another question: while we, the Slaouis, are fornicating with your mother, what are you doing, exactly, at four o'clock in the afternoon?"

Unexpectedly, Guzzler didn't react. The members of his gang stopped laughing. One of them added, in a conciliatory tone: "Uncle Ali, we're just having fun, we're not hurting anyone."

"I'm not your uncle and I don't like your idea of fun."

The final moments of the day passed by quickly. All the electrified air was diluted in the dying light. The boredom, the intolerable idleness – and with it, the desire to yell or laugh for no reason – all of it disappeared, the hospital transformed into a serene ghetto: the patients prepared their tea themselves, others went to the common room to watch television or play cards, and others walked in small groups under the trees, smoking cigarettes or looking at the sky. Rover was seated on the last step of the stairs leading to the veranda, peeling an orange.

"What did they find inside?" I asked him.

"Inside what?"

"The Moorish bathhouse."

He tossed the peel far away. After a while, he remembered, he remembered the old patriarch, a Moorish bathhouse buried in his childhood past, and a gray dawn when the police burst into the back room, next to a basin of boiling water in front of which stood Al-Haj, naked, face haggard, covered with blood.

Rover, staring at me with an almost absent look, swallowed a wedge of his orange, savoring it as if it were a madeleine. It was pointless to ask him to finish the story. I was preparing to return to my bed when he said, in a low voice, as if the memory was still fresh: "The entire family, all of them. With an axe. His three wives, the children, and the maid who had served them for years. Their mutilated bodies were marinating in the basin of boiling water."

UNTIL NOW I haven't had the chance to describe the hospital. I told myself that I would have plenty of time, it's not a place you figure out at first glance. To trace its outlines with even the broadest strokes, I would need to find out what lies beyond the trees, beyond our wing; the wings themselves (how many are there?) loom in a space that seems more indefinite and intangible to me with each passing day – space itself is being distorted in my mind because my eyes no longer perceive it in the same way. The iron gate at the main entrance was once visible at the end of the central path, between rows of ancient oaks. Now, I sometimes find myself searching for the gate from whatever spot I find myself in, as if the distance had secretly expanded during the night. Rover, who's been here so long that he's incapable of providing an exact date, only knows Wings A and B, which neighbor our own. The idea of going off to explore never occurred to him. "What's the point? There are patients everywhere, they all look the same, they all hope to one day recover and rejoin their loved ones beyond these damned high walls, but there it is, death is at the end of every road, ready to gobble us up like common flies!" Without knowing why, I convinced myself that the hospital is a trompe l'oeil, and this strange and inexplicable impression, born of a nightmare or a delirium, has yet to leave me. But whenever it becomes stubborn and intolerable in its absurdity, I chase the idea away with a torrent of logic: "So, what? Instead of healing your sad little rotting body, you're gonna abandon ship?! One of these days, you'll wake up with your brain turned completely upside down – goodbye and good night everyone, you'll go keep the jackals company, alongside the cannibals and all the other miserable devils slobbering, begging, and screaming like damned, enslaved men beaten down with clubs!"

"Okay, okay," I tell myself, "better to die on the spot than lose it little by little, but come on – this garden?"

"What garden?"

"All this vegetation around us! A caprice of a mad gardener, untroubled by aesthetics or harmony, who, on a whim of his imagination, assembled a collection of plants that have absolutely nothing in common! Look around, we're not just talking oaks, pines, palms, or harmless poplars. There's also calabash, rubber, sumac, jackfruit, manchineel, sequoia, and baobab trees, and God knows what else! Not to mention the thousands of exotic flowers that have no business in a hospital. And what's even more incredible – or don't you hear them at night? – are the countless birds everywhere, their beating wings rattling the air above our heads. And ever since (but since when?) my ears stopped capturing anything but silence, a vague buzzing of insects. Apparently streptomycin turns you deaf in the end."

"Well, better deaf than dead!"

Try as I might to concentrate, all I can hear is the faraway murmur of a town, now hostile and indifferent, and the farther still murmur of an ocean, whose heady fragrance at high tide reaches all the way to Wing C. "Today, the waves are tossing back their algae," announces Guzzler as he smells the air. "The beach is a dumping ground full of dead starfish, shells, sometimes jellyfish, I bet there'll even be a beautiful drowned body on the sand tonight!" What an odd fellow, I think. When Guzzler's not with his gang, he's a fragile, pitiful teenager, a poor kid who's never, I'm sure of it, experienced, except in his imagination, any exploits in the no man's land near the city slums. He leans against one of the veranda walls, spits with force and spite. "Guys like us don't get better! No way, guys like us do not get better. They resuscitate our small, miserable spark of life just enough that people don't quite mistake us for human beings. They tell us, hey, see you next time, and we go back to our daily bullshit, we try to return to the thick of things, we slip, we fall flat on our faces on the sidewalk, it's always too late to start living, always …" I stand up. I feel like walking. Guzzler asks me for a cigarette. "You're right to leave," he tells me. "When I'm depressed, I'm contagious." I hand him my pack of Casa Sport Olympics, he looks at it, disappointed, and scowls: "No thanks, I'm allergic to crappy smokes." He rolls downs one of his socks, takes out a pack of Marlboros. He looks at me and starts to chuckle for no reason. "Do you know why I'm laughing?"

"No."

"It's a completely idiotic memory. One time this quack came to our neighborhood to sell some pills, which, according to him, could heal every ailment, especially impotence. A single pill, he used to say, could give a dead man a hard-on for twenty-four hours, and he'd flex his arm up to his elbow. Once, we pushed him into a corner and forced him to swallow every one of his pills. He must be pissing blood to this day!" Then he adds as he lights his cigarette: "We should stuff all these bullshit shots up the doctor's ass, we'll see if he can walk after that!" I move away. Vertigo takes me. I shouldn't stay in the sun. I backtrack. Guzzler is sniffing something blackish wrapped in a piece of paper.

"It's junk," he announces like a connoisseur. "It's worth nothing at all."

"And yet you're the asshole who palmed it off on me!" protests Rover.

"Well, I was fucking with you. Go fuck yourself!"

Everything here loses its urgency. We've all become impassive, like statues unaware of the relentless accumulation of the dust of days. Instead of stretching, my notion of space hardens, contracts. Very quickly I get used to the idea that from now on we will be alone, trapped in a gigantic spider's web that thickens around our heads. In this insignificant part of the universe we are happy to move about with pointless gestures, with patchwork dreams, with conversations often had only for the pleasure of hearing our own voices. Our bodies no longer have a mission to fulfill, except to inhale the maximum amount of oxygen for our sick lungs, to accustom our clogged ears to unimportant or absurd noises, like the fart or burp of a relaxed roommate, blissfully happy as a dog, and our eyes to see only the things that bother entering our line of sight. Boredom atrophies the imagination. I'm overcome ad nauseam by the banality of my thoughts. Thankfully, spasms grab hold of me. I'm like a wild horse imprisoned in a serene body where life beats despite the fear, despite the threat of one day being diluted like a common solution in the murderous hospital air.

I SINK INTO the bed as if it were a viscous trough. My body, trapped between two slopes, doesn't move. I can't turn onto either side or the pains will return. In an effort to amuse myself, while I wait for sleep, I often localize each ache and assign an individual color to it. The shooting pain gnawing at my right side is a deep crimson; the one on my left, turquoise blue; the twinges budding in the hollows of my armpits are alternately yellow, pale green, Indian red, ocher, purple, and indigo; the areas that endure multiple syringe injections each morning are monochromatic landscapes, one single color in infinitely varying tones. Over time, I transform into an immeasurable palate unabsorbed by the night. I glow bright as a star, I rise above the room to a place where I can barely hear my companions' breathing or snoring, I gently flatten myself against the cold ceiling, turn around so that I can look down upon the beds; the void that grows between the ground and my body is so frightening that I return to my immobility in the trough. I sink into my memories in search of my youthful corpse. All I need for the past to shed its shroud, to slip on the rags of my six-year-old self, is a whiff of Brazilian coffee, a tune from a music box, or a fine drizzle falling in bright sunlight like at a jackal's wedding. But there are no scents anywhere, no scents of childhood, no scents of once abundant fruits (mulberries, carob pods, pomegranates, black nightshade berries), of wild flowers, of the sacred plants from our stories (thyme, basil, henna, laurel). Where can I find, even in my dreams, a field of poppies and ripe cornstalks gently shaken by an autumn wind? Rover emerges from a silent thunderstorm. He laughs and slaps his thighs: "You want to know if the ocean is nearby? Nothing could be easier! You follow this path of cacti until you reach palm trees, you turn left and you start down a dusty trail, which leads to the head doctor's residence. It's a large windowless villa surrounded by fir trees. If by extraordinary chance his guard dog doesn't rip off your leg or ass cheek, then that can only mean one thing: there's no longer a head doctor at this hospital. You keep tearing down the hill, and you'll arrive at the edge of a fifty-foot cliff. Then you can, if you insist, go for a nice little dip!" Guzzler appears in his turn, shoving Rover, who crumbles like dried clay: "You think that people like us can afford the luxury of memories, a past with clean diapers, notebooks, a pencil case, and a backpack? I was barely out of my mother's vagina when my childhood went up in smoke. My old man broke so many rods over my skull that it was impossible for me to get through primary school; I became an apprentice tailor, an assistant repairman of every machine ever created, I even secretly married a widow so I could have cigarettes and pocket money like a proper daddy's boy. Then, after an eternity of unemployment and begging, I started the back-and-forth hospital cycle ... So what do you call childhood or adolescence? A fancy Sunday suit, that's what!" Meanwhile, Rover has pulled himself back together, piece by piece. He coughs, vomits blood, laughs, and wipes his eyes. Guzzler hands him a Marlboro, and suggests, "Try and get yourself some good hash!" He turns to me: "Do you want Rover dead?"

"No."

"Then don't ever stop him from lying! Lies have become second nature to him. Did he already tell you the story about the old fool who chopped up everyone in his bathhouse? You haven't heard anything yet. Go ahead, Rover, how does it go again, the one about the guy who buys Al-Buraq at the Medina flea market? Not a two-bit engraving, mind you, but the real thing, the Prophet's steed, go on, tell him."

"Come on, Guzzler, another time. Can't you see that our friend is already asleep? Leave him be."

WOULD IT SURPRISE you if I said that one day I transformed myself into a spider, a weeping willow, and a cyclamen flower? Would you help me unravel my tangle of memories? Not likely. One doesn't enter a sleeping man's brain with impunity, not unless you're a brave head louse or a moonbeam. I can no longer remember the weeping willow or the cyclamen. For that matter, I doubt I ever really had branches that hung out over the sacred waters of the Ganges or the Nile, or the bloody waters of the Tigris and the Euphrates. To avoid being caught red-handed, I may as well admit that I don't know much about botany, and so I will just barely tolerate being compared to a prisoner condemned to invent his paradise behind four walls. I dreamed up my cyclamen without any preexisting knowledge: the flower therefore reflects both my ignorance and my stubborn memories that refuse to be put back together, no doubt imagined memories of something close to an ivy or poppy or maybe also a rhododendron. On the whole, we're talking about a stolen life, its weight in gold issued in counterfeit money, written in clotted blood and urine. But I had to get rid of the spider. Its toxic memory was poisoning my nights, splitting my brain with extraordinary violence. Was it my dream? Was it the spider's dream? It doesn't matter. The dream – I should say the nightmare because it haunted me for a very long time – would follow me like a curse and yet, each time it came to life, I experienced it with every fiber of my soul; quite often, at the end, I would feel distraught, vulnerable – and I wasn't ashamed to cry. How long did this last? Time during childhood is so uncertain. Later I learned that time was an adult invention, used to delineate the traps in which we struggle like small insects, or giants broken between heaven and earth. At twilight, at the exact moment when the swallows stopped fighting in the final rays of the setting sun, the house with the slatted shutters where my parents moved after my birth suddenly became a temple of exaggerated proportions; shadow-filled depths revealed mammoth caves, the staircase assaulted a sky that came down to rest on the veranda – clouds sparkling with dew and stars burning like embers – offering me an exceptional playground in which I would conceive of my small companions, sickly, underfed creatures, bald or with a single tuft of hair atop their heads, torn jackets, shoes too big for their feet. I don't know what became of those creatures. One night I found myself alone. All around me I felt the frenzy of my young body, the tingling at the roots of my hair, the beating of my bleeding heart, swollen with bitterness and sorrow, flashes of heat, fire, between my legs. Whenever it suddenly rained down ice water on the deserted street, whose residents quickly forgot about the frozen beggars sheltered under makeshift tarps or tattered pieces of burlap, I would observe these dirty and mute landscapes through the windowpanes. My eyes would follow the wildly streaming rivulets laden with paper, mud, and dead rats, and I got the feeling – or the conviction – that the world was dead, that spring was dead, that my tales, my marvelous legends, my countrysides as golden as warm pieces of cornbread were dead. Fat flies flattened themselves against the windowpanes, chased by the torrents of rain. Armed with a needle, I took malicious pleasure in skewering them one by one, their diaphanous wings buzzing in my cruel silence. They would continue to writhe and contort their thin, hairy legs as I shut them away in a matchbox. This game, which I admit I enjoyed, came to an end when my grandmother took me away one morning, of which I retain only the partial memory of another veranda, in a nearby neighborhood, where an ageless old man was holding court, surrounded by basil and sunflowers. Other children, crouched attentively, listened to him. In a serenely calm voice, he spoke of a taciturn end to the world: "On that day, all the stars in the universe will roll into infinity like rags or balls of yarn." He added: "Heaven and hell are separated by a thread so fine that it's invisible to the naked eye!" My sojourn in this camphor-infused mythology came to an end when the old man from another century died. That's when the dream of the spider began. No doubt it was a revolt on my part – a mild revolt without noise or fury – during which I doggedly began to weave my webs almost everywhere in the house with the slatted shutters. Neither of my parents seemed to notice anything unusual. For them, I was the sickly boy, the baby born two months premature in the bleak cold. I diligently took medications that made me want to vomit. I treated myself for some unknown illness. Admittedly, I had trouble breathing: I carefully avoided sleeping with my head buried under the blanket in the same way I avoided washing my face in the sink. I felt more comfortable in the spider's skin, freer in my movements. I was happy. I lived in the corners, like a Quranic schoolteacher, distracting myself while bombs, massacres, executions, and famines were plaguing the outside world. I slept a lot. Even if a careless gnat were to shake the fibers of my web, I rarely troubled myself. Dipterans are so stupid that they'd get themselves tangled in my gummy trap, rendering all movement or escape impossible. I lived like this for a long time, on the margins of a strange childhood, my monstrosity protecting me with its extraordinary warmth. I hated the tick-tock of the alarm clock, the morning cries of the street peddlers and knife sharpeners, I hated dawn when the town shook off its last dreams like a lazy donkey getting back on its feet to begin another hellish cycle of forced labor. The calls of the *muezzins* would stab like daggers at the edge of my insomnia, marking the rupture of my gentle arachnid dreams. The return to my human form transpired painfully. I would cling to the slatted shutters, trembling, feverish, gasping for air like a fish out of water. I was reborn, quite despite myself, in a worn down universe, amid a vanquished, humiliated humanity, resigned to an absurd destiny of flowering graves that led to an uncertain future in intolerable paradises. I was heading toward a mythology of survival, leaving behind in my rotting limbs a prehistory of one thousand and four hundred years of hate, vainglory, and putrid nostalgia, under the clear sky of a false Andalusia where our murder has been in the making since our birth. Many years later … the sun had gone out, unless it was just an ordinary light bulb emitting a pallid glow, without warmth, in an icy room where a monotonous voice said: "Listen to me, listen up – and stop coughing! – your body needs a specific treatment, your kneecaps are as empty as neatly cleaned seashells, they're having a hard time supporting your weight even though you're as light as a measly feather. That's why – don't cough, I said! – you're at the mercy of any gust of wind. More than one reckless soul like yours has been carried away during a quiet storm! That's why you're here now. You'll never know if you're dreaming or not. Either way, your reality doesn't matter, it's just like an autumn leaf, the slightest breeze and it will crumple in on itself and get dragged along the ground until it's completely disintegrated. Your new life isn't as bad as all that. Get used to it. Don't cough in my presence! Keep your dirty bacteria to yourself. There's one thing you need to understand, even if I have to drive it into your medieval skull with a club: you know nothing about contagion, which is normal since you don't even know that a simple device like the microscope exists. From now on you will be isolated, in another time, which will suit you wonderfully since you come from a people without schedules, who never invented so much as a butter knife!" The voice faded or continued elsewhere in a different darkness. The sun, returning, burned my retinas. It was morning, an ordinary morning, dripping like a mop, when I rediscovered with near joy the squalid backdrop of the hospital, its inhabitants, Rover and Guzzler, who were whispering on the threshold of my insomnia. "Come on, Guzzler, another time. Can't you see that our friend is already asleep, leave him be! He's in a dream that doesn't belong to us!"

"Don't leave!" I cried. "Don't leave me alone, I'm not dreaming anymore. I'm really here, with you. I'm tired of a past filled with unending rain. I no longer have the strength to find shelter there. It won't do any good anyhow." I stop talking. No one will hear me. I need to settle the score with my irreverent childhood once and for all. Forever rid myself of the divine corpse that taunts me across ten thousand layers of memory. I tell myself that once it's been cracked, no deity, whatever form it may take, can be stitched up the way you stitch up a sock, otherwise it would become something grotesque soaked in banned alcohol and mint tea. At the hospital, as in prison, religious fervor is rivaled only by the fear of being suddenly taken away to meet your maker. "This is why, you bunch of assholes, we have to tend to our ablutions every day, you could be summoned to the seventh heaven at any moment! I'm not asking you to perfume yourselves like an old lady or a queer, but all the same, be presentable, make sure your asses aren't covered in shit, make sure your armpits and feet don't stink. Our angels are, as you know, very sensitive beings. The slightest fart could have the catastrophic consequences of a tear-gas grenade." So says a patient, somewhere between a fig and a raisin, whose neck looks like a chicken that's been skinned alive. "That's Fartface," Rover tells me. "A permanent resident of Wing A. It's normal if you haven't seen him before. No hospital wall can keep him from leaving or stop him from getting back into his bed."

Guzzler goes on: "He's incurable. The doctors use him as a guinea pig, that's why he can move about as he pleases." Nobody knows Fartface's true name or age. He's the only one who wears a short-sleeved *djellaba* over his blue pajamas, also the only one to own a lute, which he wields every so often like a real troubadour. Sometimes he looks at his instrument the way you'd look at a sewing machine. Then he starts to sing. His repertoire consists of old songs from the 30s and 40s. His masters: Sheikh al-Anka, Houcine Slaoui, Raoul Journo. I was very quickly accepted into his entourage. He offered me a glass of tea and said: "We don't have last names here or even first names. We're all alike, scrawny corpses that wouldn't satisfy even a maggot. But you're not illiterate, so maybe one day you'll write a book about us, about our testicles, about the beautiful shit that we're drowning in. If it helps you overcome the passing time and daily monotony, write, for the fun of it, to piss off the world of neckties and hypocrisy, otherwise shove it down the toilet and flush three times, and when your scribblings disappear in the gurgling of the earth, say amen and go stuff yourself with suppositories until the dogs are dead!"

THIS MORNING IT'S raining dirty dishwater. The ground's become a bog that we have to wade across to get from one wing to the next. Actually all connection to the outside world appears to be severed. The other patients are so distracted by the biting cold that they haven't noticed that the nurse and his squeaking gurney are missing. The most alert among them must be thinking, "Oh, he'll pass by another time!" The windows of the neighboring block – whose uniform facade rises over the high, thick hospital wall – are all closed, locked up. No life is visible inside. Normally I can see women hanging their laundry from clotheslines stretched between television antennas, and young girls hidden behind the shutters, watching the street scene below; often I hear their radios blaring music and news of a world that's no longer my own. Now, the building looks like a stone face with lots of closed eyes, and the rain beats against it intermittently, as if to rattle its lethargy, to awaken a breath of life – but all in vain. A heavy melancholy reigns everywhere, in the traces of the ocean air. The silence of the birds and the immobility of the oak trees in the neighborhoods near Wing C remind me of a petrified forest; shrubs, thickets, branches, frozen overnight, seep, drop by drop, to the rhythm of a deluge that batters the hospital's isolated wings in slow motion. The cold is all the more intense now that we're inert. Our stiff, aching limbs grow more and more numb. And the damn heater doesn't work! Just a shitty electric hot plate hanging above the room's entrance ... but good God, why can't they just replace it? Most of the patients are coughing even harder. Rover bursts into the room, using an unfurled newspaper as an umbrella. He sits on the edge of my bed.

"It's never worked," he says.

"What?"

"The damn heater."

"What's the point then?"

"Here, this will warm you up."

He reveals, as if by magic, a paper cup of black coffee that's still hot. I take it with both hands to warm my fingers, which are starting to turn blue. He takes a cigarette out of my pack, lights it, and announces out of nowhere that he's leaving the hospital, tomorrow; then seeing the surprised expression on my face, he adds: "For a day."

"One day?"

"Come on. You think they handed me a medical certificate with 'permanently rehabilitated' written out in bold, capital letters?"

He smiles. A small, bitter smile.

I congratulate him like an idiot.

"It's nothing. They granted me one day to attend my mother's funeral."

No trace of sadness or grief in his eyes. He's watching curls of smoke rise from his cigarette.

"You're surprised that I don't look upset?" – I remain silent because I can't find anything to say – "I cried a long time ago when I was six or seven years old. Back then, my old man was drinking himself to death. The last time, he didn't get a chance to sober up. A truck ran him over. My mother didn't even respect the obligatory forty-day mourning period ..."

As he talks, I remember the dream where he crumbled like dried clay.

"You're not pulling my leg, I hope?"

He shakes his head no, several times.

"Swear on the Quran," I insist.

"A pile of Qurans won't bring her back this time. I admit, on a few occasions I've killed an imaginary aunt, an uncle, and my mother once or twice, just to get out of here. But today, I had nothing to do with it ..."

"How did you find out?"

"From a nurse who lives in our neighborhood."

He stands up, makes as if to leave, doubles back, and asks me if I need anything from town.

I suddenly realize that I no longer need anything at all from the outside world.

He lifts the wet newspaper above his head. In the doorway, he turns back toward me.

"She really is dead and I don't feel anything. I buried the woman who was my mother on the day she remarried. An old friend of my dad's was the one who took care of me when I got sick. I haven't seen her since."

He disappears behind the curtain of rain.

IT RAINED ALL day long barring a few brief moments of sunshine, respites when the daylight became glaring, so bright and colorless that it was almost blinding. In the far distance, a muffled ambulance siren rose into a metallic sky before being diluted by the echoes in a vast silence that accentuated, in periodic waves, the ephemeral signs of urban life, the intermingling of passing cars, beeping horns, crying children, and roosters crowing well after the day's first call to prayer. So, I told myself, somewhere there still exists a city with bistros, with crowded boulevards, with inhabitants obstinately playing the lotto or betting on horses. Nervous laughter drew me back to the room; someone with a falsetto voice asked if it was winter or spring, to which someone else responded, from the other side of the room: "Don't worry about it, kid, we'll send you a telegram!" Then, in the commotion that followed, another voice answered in all seriousness: "There's only a few days left before Ramadan."

"So, my good man, would you like us to start preparing you a nice little soup?!"

"Oh yeah! Would you like chicken giblets or maybe ...?"

"Patience, gentlemen, the cook's not back from the market yet."

"Hey, guys, joking aside, it's already past noon."

There were volunteers that day – Guzzler, some members of his gang, and the Arabic teacher-lookalike – who jumped out of their beds, perked up all of a sudden. The idea of fasting at lunchtime didn't appeal to them. After trading insults about the hospital treasurer – "corpse eater, orphan robber, no-good scavenger of the people" – the group set out on a mission. The table was set on the veranda with uncustomary enthusiasm, a joyful celebration in response to the morning's lethargy, a general feeling of abandon and of being forgotten during an unusually violent storm, which had transformed the wing into a small island full of shipwrecks within a hospital outside of time. They whistled, they sang, they coughed, they joked, they helped a few of the elderly patients stand up, wrapping them in dark coats, they told the others not to move: "You'll be served like at a hotel!"

It was incredible. Not so long ago an atmosphere of despair and degradation had reigned, where I saw nothing around me but sick, motionless men huddled up in the cold, doomed to misery and a niggling death; but now I too felt myself come alive as if I were in a village of trappers and miners, on the summit of an Oregon mountain transplanted to the High Atlas, populated by Berbers and penned in by a rude winter. Instinctively, survival became organized. Some of the residents – the ones from the country – promised to collect wood and light a bonfire. Add violins and tambourines to the mix and the illusion of a lively celebration would have been complete. Even the storm obliged, diminishing in intensity. It was during a tolerable drizzle that Guzzler and his companions reappeared with a large cooking pot and place settings; the teacher-lookalike carried a breadbasket protected under a plastic tablecloth. They were welcomed by heartfelt applause and cheering, in honor of the courageous explorers who had braved the bad weather and defied the hospital staff's indifference. I barely ate. Guzzler emptied my plate onto his own. "You got dinner reservations tonight?" His mouth full, he laughed and jeered. Someone was soliloquizing about the benefits of the rain – it was the man who had been talking about Ramadan, a tall, thin guy with a dubious-looking turban knotted around his watermelon-shaped head. Guzzler, annoyed, turned toward him.

"Fine, Grandpa, the rain may be a blessing from God, but explain to me why fruits and vegetables are getting more and more expensive!"

"Maybe because now they're imported from faraway in America!" hammed up one patient, prompting his neighbor to raise his voice to the same level.

"Well, I think it's the rain's fault! It falls where it shouldn't, here for example, solely to bug the hell out of us."

"Thanks be to God and be careful about insulting the rain!"

Across from me, the food-stand owner lifted his head. He pushed his empty plate aside and said in a categorical tone, without addressing anyone in particular, that it was a question of politics.

"Which politics?" asked Guzzler without looking at him. "Now potatoes and fava beans are political?"

"Political or not," interjected a guy from Wing A, "I haven't had a banana or apricot in so long that I've forgotten how they taste!"

Everyone around the table lost it, gesticulating, sputtering, lips rolled back from their toothless mouths, eyes yellow and gleaming, Adam's apples twitching in their frenzied throats, furiously evoking the fruits of their childhoods: cherries, raspberries, peaches, mangoes, Muscat grapes, apples, pears, plums, currants, pineapples ...

"What the hell do you know about pineapples? You've never even eaten one!"

"Exactly! That's why I mentioned it."

"There's nothing but pumpkins where you come from!"

"Better a pumpkin than esparto grass!"

"Even prickly pears, which used to be free, are sold like pastries now – one at a time!"

A high voice rang out above the fray. Guzzler leaned toward me to murmur that "the Brother" was going to deliver his sermon reserved for special occasions.

"Why do you call him the Brother?"

"Because he's always got his nose stuck in some journal from the Middle East, but don't kid yourself, he reads Arabic about as well as I read Chinese."

I listened to the sermon for a moment. If the Brother was to be believed as he thundered before this tribe of pagans, we should have been thanking God every second of every day and night, for each breath, each burp, each fart.

"Hold on, Brother!" Guzzler interrupted abruptly. "Turn down your dial a little, you're keeping me from digesting in peace."

The tall, bearded guy shot him a look charged with at least two hundred volts, followed by a diatribe that covered, haphazardly, Sodom and Gomorrah, the lost people of Lot, and the Second World War when Europeans fed themselves on maggots and rats, "because they lost the faith a long time ago and they're doomed to the eternal flames of Gehenna!" This prompted Guzzler to cry out like a damned man: "Here's to hell then!" As everyone shouted themselves hoarse, laughing until they cried, and after the Brother cursed us all before slipping out, Guzzler said, looking to me for support: "Well shit! Ever since we first set eyes on this world, without even enough time to cut the umbilical cord, they've been drumming all the worst calamities into us, day and night. Don't do this, Mohamed! Don't do that, Mohamed! Not in public! Get on your knees and pray, even if it means cracking your spine. Enough! Fuck it. Somebody bring me a barrel of wine, some sliced meat and cheese, and a glass of mahia liquor on the double! There's only one hell, the true one, and it's where we spend all our days – here. It's right here!"

"May God bless the hell where we spend all our days – here!" chanted the members of his gang in unison, pounding their fists on the table; others kept the beat with knives and forks, and the rest, leaning their chairs against the wall, danced to exhaustion. A clap of thunder suddenly rang out, then a downpour fell from the sky, drenching the revelers on the veranda, who scattered like a herd of bison. A few seconds later, nothing remained of the celebration: the rain pounded down on the large table strewn with litter and breadcrumbs, which were dispersed pitifully across the tiles by pellets of water. Around four o'clock, I took advantage of a lull and rejoined Guzzler and his gang in one of the bedrooms. Fartface, kneeling on his bed like an officiant, was singing the final verses of *El Marikane*, playing along with his lute.

During every chorus, he lifted up his chin – with its thin, salt-and-pepper goatee – and everyone repeated in unison: "zee Americans," placing heavy emphasis on the "z." Tea was handed out around the circle. Fartface delicately placed his lute against the wall and demanded a cigarette, which was immediately handed to him, already lit. He took one, two long drags, which he exhaled through his nostrils, then said, as if he was continuing a speech that had been interrupted: "Last night I thought that was it. I was stretched out as stiff as a board, I was even cursing myself for having forgotten the candles, yeah, I know, it's hard to believe but I'm attached to the candles, you can't deny there's a certain panache to a dead body surrounded by flames. Then I recited the profession of faith – one, two, three, four, five times, you never know – and I closed my eyes, and I waited. After a while, I glanced at my watch, then closed my eyes again, and waited, on and on."

"And he came?" asked Guzzler, flopped on the ground.

"Things like this only ever happen to me! So I'm waiting to meet the Big Boss, happily imagining the scene here, when you all discover my lifeless body and tear at the skin on your faces, sobbing like grieving mothers-in-law, and that's when I hear a rumbling, then something like toads croaking in a pond; I lift up my head one more time, wondering if the storm didn't leave some of the nasty creatures near the veranda. But I had to face the facts, it was my insides gurgling like crappily assembled pipework. Worse! Me, who had taken the trouble to perform the necessary ablutions, well, I couldn't hold it back any longer, a fart as big as a juicy melon rang out, followed by a shit I could barely restrain. I ran to the toilet like a maniac and nearly fell flat on my back in the dark – and there you have it! Something like this had to happen to me, of all people: while waiting in a religious fervor, what falls into my lap but raging diarrhea! So now I'm asking you, my friends, my only brothers in this lowly world, what do I have to do?"

"Eat lots of rice," said a young teenager we had christened Argan because he was originally from Sous.

"Asshole!" replied Fartface. "I'm not talking about my diarrhea. When I need a remedy I'll ask you for one."

Someone asked, credulously, if angels were like civil servants.

"What's your point?" said Fartface. "Everyone knows angels are the civil servants of heaven."

"And death, isn't he an angel sent from heaven too?"

"What are you getting at, runt?"

"I'm getting at this: you performed your ablutions, your nightly prayer, you recited the profession of faith, but you forgot the most important part."

"And what, according to you, is the most important part? The rest of you shut the hell up, let the runt answer."

And the runt said: "You forgot to bribe him."

Fartface, caught off guard, finally burst into laughter, so loud, so deep, so contagious, that no one could resist the desire to roll on the floor laughing, too. Guzzler, in tears, legs in the air, was kicking like a mule whose ass had been rubbed with Sudanese hot peppers. A second later, everybody was drying their eyes, hiccuping, breathing noisily like punctured bellows.

Fartface, very serious, asked: "And how much should I give him, in your opinion?"

"Twenty francs!"

"Fifty!"

"A hundred!"

"A thousand!"

"More," said Guzzler, even more serious. "In my opinion, he won't accept less than one million, given the subject isn't worth anything."

"And where am I supposed to dig up that kind of money, huh?" – Fartface pretended to look sad – "It's not by chance that I got stuck with this nickname. First off, my birth was tainted by the seal of catastrophe: food shortages, epidemics, rationing, Hitler ..."

"Ha! Now you want us to believe that you were born during the Second World War?"

"Him?! He's old as dirt!"

"Come to think of it, how old are you?"

"Yeah, really, how old are you?"

Fartface turned toward me. "Hey, Smart-Ass! I get a kick out of you writing a book about us, but be careful, not a word about what I said earlier, and whatever you do, don't mention my diarrhea, it won't leave a good impression, and come on, what will future generations think of a guy like me, huh? Okay?"

THERE'D NEVER BEEN so many seagulls in the sky. Hundreds, maybe a thousand, judging by the noise that filled the space stretching from one end of the horizon to the other. No one inside or out seemed surprised, impressed, or even worried about the incredible gathering of seagulls swarming so close to us, above the hospital, beyond the tall oaks and poplars. After multiple attempts to focus on at least a few of the particular birds that had strayed from the dense group to cross a piece of sky within my sight, I was forced to give up; on two occasions I had lost my balance on the muddy ground and nearly fallen flat on my face in the high grass that concealed treacherous puddles of rainwater. Once safely underneath my blankets, I closed my eyes and blindly tallied thousands of palmipeds as white as sea spray as they whirled above the tall silvery waves pounding the coastal roads, reaching as far as the cracked walls of the nearest houses; from the birds' fierce cries, I imagined two of them battling up there in the sky, snapping at each other like hens; no doubt a skua on the attack, I thought, forcing another gull to cough up a recently-caught fish ... "I bet there'll even be a beautiful drowned body on the sand tonight!" Guzzler had said. What I saw was my own corpse, a younger one, from the old photographs no longer good for anything, not even to make me fleetingly relive the old terror of nights filtered through candles lit along back alleys to exorcise the "sea spirits," to defend our piss-filled beds from the woman with long black hair capable of meta-morphosing into someone you loved, living or dead, to lure you into her devilish traps. This time, the vision only lasted for the bat of an eyelash. Opening my eyes, all I saw were men as miserable as me, stretched out in clammy beds, clinging to their own childhoods or coughing, spitting, and moaning in a silence that wasn't my own, a cavernous silence, out of the reach of the battles waged by my warlike seagulls as they used their beaks to frenetically tear apart the flesh of the kid I was happy to no longer be. This was when Rover materialized – in front of me, or maybe beside me, sometimes walking with an alert and rapid pace and sometimes with an awkward duck-like gait – and I laughed because he looked like a dolled-up shoeshine boy or, better yet, someone who'd been recently circumcised; he trotted along with calculated caution, avoid-ing the painful friction of his injured member against the rough fabric of his tight pants, he grimaced with each step, and, a fake smile laboriously painted on his face, his cheeks stiff and pink, he repeated: "No point in accompanying me, I know the way better than you do!" He was wearing a short-sleeved beige jacket over a badly ironed shirt with a limp col-lar and a pair of pants that stopped short of his ankles; his damp black hair was plastered to his skull with a poorly done part on the left side – the splitting image of a guy ready to stand to attention before the camera lens of a photographer specializing in what we used to call "water pictures." He'd tried to sneak out but hadn't counted on our malicious curi-osity. We were staked out along the main path, happy as hell to give him a stately escort up to the gate, dispensing our particular brand of advice: "Don't get raped on the bus!" said Guzzler. "Say hi to the virgins in your neighborhood for us."

"That is if you can still find virgins over there!"

"And bring us back some candy," yelled Argan. "Sour balls, hard candy, caramels, and a few Ferrero Rochers would be nice."

"You're crazy! He's not going to Paris, he's on his way to Amsterdam by way of the Bou Regreg, where the flies are as big as the sparrows!"

"Come back to us in one piece, kid, but if you do get raped, we have Mercurochrome to patch you up!"

Long after Rover left, I still hadn't shaken my deep depression: I was fixated on the dumb idea that our goodbye had been permanent. "Will he be able to find his way back?" Argan and Guzzler looked at me blankly. "Here, I forgot," said Guzzler as he took a wrinkled envelope out of his pocket and held it out to me. "Read what's in it aloud." Argan, impressed, barked his admiration. "It's not mine, you idiot! Do I look like someone who gets letters in the mail? An old villager from Wing A asked me to figure it out for him ..." I read it. Using a series of traditional, ready-made formulas written by the village *fkih*, a worried woman prayed for that old man's quick recovery and spoke of her eldest, ungrateful son, who had sold their cow to travel to a distant country whose name was impossible to remember.

My two friends left me alone. I sat down on a bench, under the trees. My heart was beating quickly, as if I'd been running all morning. Rover had been gone for half an hour. All I could see now was a large cat, frozen like a statue, in the same spot where he'd taken off to escape our sarcastic taunts; it was probably one of the neighborhood cats that no fence could prevent from reaching the large hospital trashcans. At this very moment Rover is making his way through a dense and noisy crowd, after rushing off a bus whose passengers seem horrifyingly unreal through its steamed up windows. Right now, he's standing in front of his childhood home with the despair of someone who's completely lost, trying to recognize a door with a bronze knocker, a low building with windows so minuscule he can't imagine what purpose they could serve, a place that once observed him growing up on thin grasshopper legs, the neighbors' oddly horizontal stairs, dark and stinking of urine and weak stew, which in a faraway time provided a refuge for a romantic idyll; his brain refuses to reconstruct the facial features of a young girl with braids. He stops, he doesn't recognize where he is – or only barely – and nobody recognizes him. I don't know why but in my imagination it's pouring rain. By chance or by prophesy, it's raining drops as big as light bulbs, which melt onto the crumbling cobblestones, street stalls, boutiques, old carts, and pack animals of this microcosm that I can't tame, which I want to study in detail, giving it a semblance of life despite my ignorance. "Don't tire yourself out," Rover tells me. "Your landscapes are toying with you, teasing you. You see me in pale daylight that will darken soon enough, I'm as substantial as a watercolor in the rain, my outline is disappearing already, look at me oozing, trickling away in rivulets, it's best to leave me alone, let me manage my own ghosts, angels, and ogres! Stay away, old man, my business is mine alone. People don't get visitors in their graves you know!" Seated on a bench, under the trees, nothing can tear me away from my quiet serenity. The years go by, sowing wrinkles, white hair, disease, and forgetfulness. I'm no longer thinking about anything, I can no longer think. I'm frozen like that large cat, happy as a fool, indifferent to the changes in the seasons. The sun, warm as a

Moorish bath set to its maximum temperature; a gust of wind laden with sea spray; a second gust filled with swirling dead leaves, then, once again, the Chergui, sand, dust, and water. Nothing makes a dent in my skin, which now resembles that of a tortoise. A tree with buds is pushing, growing, winding through the tips of my fingers, my knees, along my spinal column, and in my head, slowly spreading through my dried-out veins to conquer my innermost depths. There's no use. I don't have roots. Nothing but ink cap mushrooms sprouting from my ears, nostrils, and weeping eyes. Through my tears, in a halo, I see Guzzler, Argan, Fartface, and my other friends. They haven't aged a day; as they smile at me in their awkward manner, I can see their concern, incomprehension, muted question marks, and a range of expressions that I'm unable to define, that's how much my head – heavy and trapped in the jaws of a vise, in a circle of dizziness – is preventing me from seeing the pitiable reality in which I'm lost. Someone places a hand on my forehead, then a voice says: "Are you okay?" I straighten up on one elbow. "Of course I'm okay, what's gotten into you guys?"

"Well, what's with you, huh, staying out in the rain?" Guzzler says.

"What rain? Is it still raining in my head? Where's Rover? The last time I saw him, he liquefied into colors."

People are moving around me, barely listening to me. I'm naked under the blankets. I touch myself: no mushrooms, no flower buds, the tree has deserted my feverish body. Where's my tree? Someone brings me my pajamas and helps me put them on. The fabric gives off the pleasant smell of eucalyptus; the smell is strong, it permeates the space around me, chasing away all the other clammy odors: hyenas, jackals, rabbit holes, fenugreek, and rancid butter. It's still daytime – but which day? A wood fire burns at the wing's entrance, encircled by seated and standing shadows. So, I tell myself, the country boys kept their promise. The pleasant feeling of a makeshift camp reigns once again and the only thing missing is the intoxicating fragrance of bread baked with cow pats and the song of cicadas under a sky blazing with stars. In the glow of the nearby lights of the invisible town, our foggy sky is an immense, crinkled burlap cloth, lacking celestial bodies, lacking a Milky Way, a palette of drab colors whose scale of grays triumphs over the setting sky's vague streaks of red-crimson.

"You're here thanks to the on-duty nurses. They found you sitting on the bench, in the rain, like one of those Hindu dervishes who thinks himself a mineral. Luckily it was just a drizzle. Next time you feel like taking a bath in a thunderstorm, I'll lend you my best umbrella!"

"And I'll give you the coat Smalto gave me for my birthday!"

We all laugh, Guzzler, Argan, and me, seated on the steps outside our wing, next to the bonfire. Within this circle of flickering light, the hunched shadows remind me of the Easter Island giants.

GOOD GOD, WHAT the hell am I doing here? It's the thousandth time I've asked myself this question, like some idle traveler who's visiting a place where boredom very quickly becomes insufferable. "That's why you're here today. You will never know if you're dreaming or not. Either way, your reality doesn't matter!" I still hear this voice from the past. The head doctor, senior nurse, or one of the orderlies – unless it was someone I invented, influenced by my readings of Kafka, Borges, and Buzzati in my youth ... no, it was definitely someone real – from our reality – who had forbidden us from coughing in his presence – as if we were coughing just for the fun of it – and reproached us with his military sergeant voice for not having invented the microscope or the butter knife.

"Are we really a people?" – Now Fartface is sputtering away – "Think about it. We were born with our right hands outstretched, begging in our blood, not to mention cowardice, infamy, and fear, an insidious fear that drives us to curve our spines all the way to the ground! Fear of what, I ask you? Too much servitude has made us forget what dignity, generosity, and tolerance truly are. We don't even know how to talk anymore, our people's pitiful vocabulary barely fits in the palm of my hand, we're nothing but a bunch of poor bastards, maggots, worms, garbage on credit! And me, the guy talking to you, vomiting on you, well and truly crazy deep inside my rotting soul, puffed up with a whole lot of nothing, I'm just renting this body, waiting for someone to give me a good kick in the ass and tell me that I've swallowed too much oxygen, that my carcass is creating a traffic jam: Go on, keep moving you old slob, enough fooling around!"

"Okay Grandpa, enough fooling around!" interrupts Guzzler. "Let the cadavers have some fun. That's enough blubbering out of you. You must be really thirsty, huh? You want a glass of red wine? Chausoleil, Moghrabi, or Vieux Papes? I must have a bottle of wine around here somewhere, right? Unless you prefer a Ricard, a double scotch? With or without ice? Dry? Like Humphrey Bogart! Very well, sir! At your service, sir!"

Using a towel as an apron, Argan carries an imaginary tray, and bends down to serve Fartface, who has finally flopped onto his bed.

Fartface plays along. He pretends to take the glass, shakes it, inhales like a true connoisseur, takes a sip, winces.

"Mmmn! It's the real thing. I bet it comes from Scotland! No one's ever called me 'sir' before. Is that included in the price of the drink or the tip?"

I shrink into my corner. I wonder, again one time too many, what I'm doing here. It's an odd cemetery whose residents live above the graves, among the brambles, cacti, insects, reptiles, poppies, and jonquils, they move around in blue two-piece shrouds, wearing slippers or babouches, a heap of insults perched on their chapped lips, drooling from the corners of their mouths. And here I am among them, a voluntary prisoner, indolent, more lethargic than anyone, lazing around, pointlessly darkening page after page. My fingers tremble, sometimes they scratch out writing that isn't mine, that I have trouble deciphering. Who will read me? My characters are cobbled together, haloed in off-the-rack dreams, drowning in deadly inertia and having solo adventures, drinking all the imaginary wine they can get their hands on, sleeping right and left with whores as beautiful as Nefertiti and Elizabeth Taylor, looking like gaunt cowboys, bandits, pirates, and gangsters suffering from chronic bronchitis, trachoma, and I don't know what other form of divine benediction. In my solitude, I call out to them, one by one:

"Fartface!"

"Present!"

"Age, profession, address?"

"No age, no profession, no address!"

"How old would you like to be?"

"Old as a donkey."

"Explain."

"Nothing to explain, dear captain! The donkey is born, and instead of thinking, he farts; instead of talking, he brays; then he lives, he lives to transport loads, to get slapped around, to get erections come spring, and he never stops to take a shit, he's always in a hurry, always servile. When he does die – he doesn't know it, he dies, that's it."

"The profession you'd like to have?

"None, God forbid."

"A good-for-nothing?"

"Oh, no, too ambitious. You see, dear captain, ever since I was born, people have told me: 'Work is the ticket to health!' So I worked, I slogged away like a slave, and one beautiful morning, I lost my health. For good. And that got me thinking. You don't make money by working up a good sweat, but by cheating, stealing, running rackets, trafficking. I'm no lawyer but I say you have to know how to read between the lines of the law. Only idiots interpret it literally, idiots and honest people, which is the same difference. That's why they built prisons, for those pour souls. When they say, 'society is well designed,' you should always ask yourself: for whom?"

"Guzzler!"
    "Here."
    "How old are you?"
    "Eighteen."
    "How do you know?"
    "My father was an accountant."
    "What's your profession?"
    "Ruffian, robber, occasional trafficker, gigolo, pimp, and when it comes to the Creator, an I-don't-give-a-shitter, to name just a few."
    "And now?"
    "I'm in between jobs, sir. Like everyone. My life is temporary, my hopes are temporary, my sleep and dreams are temporary. I am temporarily counting a lot on the future, and here, look, sir, I have a temporary work certificate for when I'll be temporarily healed."

"Argan?"
    "Yes. I get my nickname from the rarely-seen argan tree from Sous, which provides the local beggars with a dark, heavy oil that they eat morning, noon, and night."
    "Do you speak Tachelhit?"
    "I can insult and curse fluently, but on occasion I speak it very respectfully, like when I have to borrow something from the neighborhood grocer or ask for credit. He's a stingy,

hard-nosed guy, even with himself, but he's a dyed-in-the-wool regionalist ..."

"Okay, okay, that's enough!"

"And you? Yes, you. You're new!"

"Yeah ... I arrived two days ago, I think ... I don't know why, for that matter ..."

"You're not sick?"

"They didn't give me a chance to ask. There was a guy yelling 'next!' the whole time, so I followed and here I am."

"And what's your name?"

"O.K.'s my name, at least that's what my friends call me, they're Americanophiles, unconditional enthusiasts of Yankee TV shows since birth, it sounds smart and you can say it quickly, but if you want to call me Oum Kalsoum, I don't have any objections. I'm educated in literature, civics, religion, and sports. I know the *Muallaqāt* and the sixty verses of the Quran, which helps me distinguish the assholes-for-life from the *Petit Poucets*. Let me explain: the assholes-for-life never admit that it's all gibberish, all the way back to Antiquity, they don't understand a thing but they've got their stupid pride; the others have a memory like little Poucet, a verse here, a piece of the Quran there, gleaned along the way, like a trail of stale breadcrumbs leading from primary school all the way to their favorite café today. But you know what, after I left school, I found myself dragging my ass, in the mud and muck of a third category, the mystagogues of Arabic grammar, dandies who can't even be bothered to make a living typing on an Underwood keyboard! I worked one month at the Ministry of Justice and had my fill, a real lake of shit and slime full of alligators, anacondas, and piranhas with an appetite for gobbling human beings up in a fraction of a second. I had to cleanse myself in unemployment for a while to save my idealist nature, but once again I found myself dragging my ass. But no crying here, where would I get my tears from?"

"Hey, look who's back from the Southern seas! Come on, Sinbad, tell us about your seventh voyage to the land of the turbaned Mormons. How was your pilgrimage to the springs of milk and honey?" Rover blows on his hands to warm them up, his eyes glistening but not brimming over. And when he smiles, he looks like some beachcomber who'd turned over all the pebbles on the beach only to find sand and corals. "Come on, old man, tell us what's become of the outside world and the neighborhood virgins" – Rover bites his lip – "We're thirsty for noises, cries, crowds, and skies." He sighs and obstinately stops talking. It's only later that he'll share his odyssey of sadness and silence.

"HOW'S IT GOING?" "Good." "Good-good?" "Meh, so-so I guess, could be better." "The family?" "Good." "The kids?" "Good, they grow up all on their own and then get the hell out." "And the youngest?" "He had scarlet fever, measles, chicken pox, and diarrhea, but God is grand." "So, you're good, *hamdoullah*!" "And you?" "As long as you have your health ..." "Yeah, that's what my old man used to say, he'd repeat it from morning to night, until the day he started spitting up blood." "We belong to God and to him we return." "Hear, hear!" "*Mektoub*!" "Yeah, everything is *mektoub*! Everything is written. My dictionary's so big you'd need a wheelbarrow and two brawny guys to push it!" "Yeah, mine's a phone book from 1930." "Why 1930?" "That way all the addresses are old and the phone numbers are always busy." "Speaking of, what ever happened to what's-his-face?" "He's in prison." "God bless him! Now there's a fellow who never watered down his wine." "Same with the other guy – what was his name again? – who hates anyone who drinks their coffee with milk." "Oh yeah, where did he end up?" "In prison too, but at Ali Moumen or El-Ader, I don't remember." "Lucky bastard! He'll have at least a degree in agricultural engineering by the time he gets out." "I doubt it, twenty years or life, same difference. If he ever gets pardoned – you never know – the poor guy's in for a shock, his chickens will have wisdom teeth and his mule a pair of Siamese twins!"

Argan and O.K. excel at the art of talking without saying anything. Their conversations can go on for hours, and the stakes are high: a pack of Marlboros or chewing gum – it depends on the day – to whoever can keep from laughing or running out of responses. I hear their voices and sense the presence of the jury and a few others; lying in my bed, looking through dirty windowpanes, I watch the sky, a washed-out, icy sky with a small timid breeze, the promise of a storm at midnight or in tomorrow's early hours. I'm tired of watching the sky, it's giving me pits in my stomach and cramps in my brain. I open *Moravagine* at random, and read: " ... then you emerge among the Vallataons, called Jemez Indians by the Mexicans. The settlement has a Catholic church (an *estoufa* in the native tongue). The church is empty and half in ruins. It is dedicated to Montezuma, and in it a perpetual flame is kept burning in expectation of Montezuma's return, at which time he is to establish his universal empire." I close the book and I think about Blaise Cendrars. I tell him: "Take me to the end of the world!" He grabs me with his only hand and we sail around in a dugout canoe, under mangrove roots, through jungles, fogs, awful smells, we subsist on oysters and crabs in the shape of ossified anuses, and eat honey ants – Blaise tells me: "The natives are mad for the honey ant; it's a well-known aphrodisiac." Suddenly, after several pages, we berth in Paris, Boulevard Exelmans. I leave him with Moravagine at a wine shop, and I return to the room in Wing C where, for a minute or two, blue Indians dance in my eyes before fading to make way for blue pajamas coughing at almost regular intervals. Then, I sink once more into my body, surrounded by Fartface, Guzzler, Rover, Argan, and O.K., I tell them: "I can no longer see the main iron gate, or the life beyond that simmers like a sauce pot full of nasty things. I think they're building a new wall, no, I'm sure of it, and they'll construct other walls that air, space, and our dreams can't cross; only our silence will grow, fatten, swell like a mountain ..." Guzzler laughs: "Smart-Ass has lost his marbles!"

ROVER SAYS: "WHEN I arrived at the house, it was all over. An old shrew was washing the tile floor of my mother's bedroom. After pouring out buckets and buckets of brackish water that two young girls had pulled up from a well beneath the staircase, the old woman found herself wading barefoot in an actual pond. Each time she stood up straight, groaning, she would hit her head against the single light bulb hanging from the ceiling; then, after mumbling two or three unintelligible curses, damning her rheumatism, the light bulb, or the two young girls – who dawdled each time they walked to the well, whispering and squealing in the dim light – the shrew would once again pick up the mop, plunge it into the lake, pull it out, wring it into a bucket, and plunge it back in again. I stood on the doorstep, thinking it would take her until the next day to drain the water. A cold, wet breeze made me shiver. I coughed. The old woman stood up and turned toward me: 'Come help me lean the mattress against the wall.' I did, silently. Once we were done, the woman ignored me and continued to mop the room. Before leaving the house, I asked the girls for news of my stepfather – the bastard, who'd been scrounging off my mother like a leech, was probably hanging around the bars and cheap restaurants, and wouldn't return until late at night to play the tearful widower, getting a free dinner out of it from the neighbors. The harpy interrupted the girl talking to me, threatening to come after her with a club. 'It's old Aïcha's

105

son!' cried out both girls as they hurried to the funeral room holding the bucket full of water. 'What son? Aïcha only had one, and he died a long time ago!' I walked out and leaned against the front door. I coughed even harder. When I was done, I had an irresistible urge to throw up. All I could conjure up were a few tears, and a dull anger. In the alleyway, a half-naked brat was calmly watching me; behind some shutters, Mohammed Abd el-Wahab was singing *Moi qui toute ma vie n'ai jamais aimé*; a newborn began to scream as if he was being poked in the bottom with a burning hot needle. My rage fed off my inability to strangle the brat, Mohammed Abd el-Wahab, or the infant. I staggered across the alley. A woman, who'd opened her door to empty a tub full of dirty laundry water, let out a stream of insults against drunks and against policemen not doing their jobs. I went to the Salé seaside cemetery. I'd remembered a plot of land with high grass, brambles, and nettles covering old, nearly erased tombstones and, next to a small *koubba*, several recent graves covered with tiles or simply cemented over, around which men loitered, squatting, like vultures, reciting the Quran in memory of the deceased, lying in wait for the grieving visitor who would give them a handful of figs, dates, and of course coins. When I crossed through a well-worn gap in the cemetery wall and found myself before hundreds upon hundreds of graves, I knew right away that I wouldn't be able to find my mother's. I wandered there, in the silence, a heavy silence despite the monotonous surf of the nearby ocean and the piercing cries of the seagulls. Butterflies, bees, flies, and beetles fluttered fearlessly around me, landing on my head or my shoulders; a man in a straw hat appeared from behind a cairn, pulling up his pants. He took a long time to zip up his fly. When I asked where my mother was buried, he gave me an odd look before responding: 'What do you want me to tell you? It's not like I have a hotel ledger here. There are tons of clients every day and they're all the same. Can't even be bothered to buy a properly carved headstone, nope, the families are too busy setting up landmarks. Look! This isn't a cemetery, it's a dumping ground, full of plastic bottles, rags, shards of glass, pieces of wood, even ripped boxer shorts and filth stained with menstrual blood!' He yelled and spit on the ground at the same time. Instead of punching his pathetic face, I settled for asking him what he, the guardian of this respectable place, thought of those who shamelessly crap on the dead. I walked away, leaving him to freeze in his own rot. I wandered between the graves for a while, with no luck, and afterward I headed toward the fishermen on the rocks. And until sundown I kept my gaze on a boat that was struggling to get past the horizon. Returning to the house, I found the drunk snake swigging away, two plastic bottles of red wine wrapped in newspaper at his feet. He was yelling about 'his' money, the money spent on the shroud, the funeral, the food, the *tolba,* and the obligatory six feet of dirt; suddenly, he burst into tears. I was nauseated by this inebriated wreck of a man, by the acidic stench of bad wine combined with the stink of sewers and artichokes. I had to leave that house as soon as possible, and yet I couldn't move, I was almost bewitched by all this disintegration. The hospital struck me as a peaceful haven. From that moment on, going back was a question of survival. I bitterly regretted where I was, staring at this man who'd been nothing but a stranger to me, a despicable person, a slug you should crush under your heel. Now, the bad wine was once again reviving the meanness in him. His eyes glistened with hatred. 'You need cash, nowadays, to kick the bucket! You have to pay dearly to get eaten up by maggots! And his highness the grave-digger doesn't bargain, no sir! His prices are set like at the big boulevard stores! That corpse eater sure knows how to fuck us over, you only die once, you know, and God is watching, up high, unfazed, though for that matter I wonder if He's still there!' The old cretin let his head fall on his chest, like it was dislocated. I figured he'd suddenly fallen asleep. I was preparing to leave when he straightened up and showered me with insults. He tried to stand up with the intention of strangling me, but his legs buckled. He collapsed in a heap and stopped moving. I spit on him and left, slamming the door shut once and for all. Outside, it was a beautiful and chilly day."

WITH RAMADAN CAME the first real signs of deterioration. Fear and a profound anxiety in the patients' cobwebbed minds resurrected the powerful hold of prostration and resignation in what was a heavy and cruel centuries-old routine. Though the season's light was familiar to everyone – blinding at times, with an unbearable heat – we all lost ourselves within it. When dusk came like a breath that lasted until darkness settled in, my own sun – pitiful shattered mirrors, pieced back together – fell in ruins around me, trapping me in unanswered questions. A prisoner of the hospital or my body, stripped of everything, even my memory; I once had the power to mold myself out of clay as I wished, in the blood of stars and legends, in the flavor of a thousand springs and gentle winters filled with songs and nursery rhymes since buried in secret creases; I slept and woke with frightening feelings of inconsistency and dread, of being torn apart, of no longer being guided by a logical thread. My descent into the muddy ruts of day and night cruelly reproduced a distorted, gruesome image of victory and freedom.

Regardless of where I look, even in the depths of my sleep, I see nothing but men decaying faster than ever before. It's not just disease wearing them down. A new curse – is that the right word? – gnaws at their livers, hearts, arteries, and testicles, permanently tattooing their yellow pupils with a gaze even more distraught than that of a child who no longer has a childhood; disoriented, walking, or staggering in a spatial plane without bearing or direction, they stop, hesitant, suddenly blind, asking themselves if they should double back, advance, or remain motionless – like scarecrows abandoned in the middle of a vast empty field – then, spurred on by a sudden burst of energy, harried by the heat emanating from the thousand mouths of hell, they take refuge under their sheets, hidden away, festering, sticky with sweat that's far worse than any ordinary fever, haunted by nightmares, mouths opened, throats wheezing, ignoring or unaware of the gray flies stuck to their eyelashes, teeth, and tongues. Their misery – more crushing than a death multiplied over and over, a failed death, reviving itself with all the cruelty of a rusted knife – is well and truly the misery of a devout believer no longer able to answer to God's whims.

I don't want to trap myself inside the idea of an inevitable and suicidal unhappiness. I cling to the freedom of the cloud – an uncertain freedom subject to the vagaries of the wind – a freedom that sometimes forms and dissipates so quickly that I barely have time to make out a mountain or an immense tortured face, a detail hurriedly torn from a fresco that looks like *Guernica* or a Hieronymus Bosch painting. Now that I think about it, my most distant memories – as lifelike as my spider dreams – go back to those timeless days when, stretched out on the veranda of my childhood home (the house with slatted shutters forever closed) or perhaps in the distant and legendary Anonymous Hills where I spent my vacations with my grandmother Yamna, my eyes drunk with infinity, my small selfish heart, avoiding the daily worries and fears of ordinary men (insufficient food, lack of money, diseased animals, drought, or simply a sales slump at the weekly souk), didn't imagine clouds auguring good weather, but rather mobile structures drawn with nervous, careless brushstrokes: pagodas, cathedrals, Saharan casbahs, minarets pierced with wooden stakes emerging from the skies over Asia, the West, or perhaps an Incan America, or from more familiar skies above Timbuktu or a sandstorm-struck Smara. Sometimes, the fruits of my nocturnal terrors would also stretch from one end of the horizon to the other: impossible giants, made of water and thunder, with the wings of a thousand birds, beaks and talons gleaming, and rainbows, crowns, and sabers from universal mythologies, or else forbidden, bloody kingdoms of laughing, grimacing, or serene deities, rotting since time immemorial under apocalyptic hurricanes, tropical vegetation crawling with wart-covered monsters, and living dunes carved from colossal rocks on which tenacious erosion will never take hold.

Impossible to escape my current condition for long. My visions quickly disappear as the men in white enter; they materialize amid the howls of an enraged pack, envious of our prerogatives as infidel worshipers of fire or false idols, mark the occasion by calling us – these are their favorite insults – happy miscreants disrespectful of the ancestral religion. Their jokes on the first day of Ramadan rarely vary, something like "Come on, you gluttons, stand up, prepare your butt cheeks!" or else, "No luck today, nothing but roasted chicken and pastilla!" and they roar with laughter each time a shriveled old man, shy or ashamed, nervously but persistently inquires whether our medications, liquid or pill, will unavoidably violate his fast. Nothing surprises me anymore, not since my conversation with the head nurse who offhandedly told me, in a bored and jaded tone, that dozens of patients would die during this "sacred month." "Listen to me, young man, no matter what the suited up *muftis* on television say nowadays, medicine and religion are incompatible. Let them come take a look here themselves, they'll see toilet stalls strewn with hastily discarded pills, not to mention everything that's been flushed down to the sewers!"

"But can't you tell the sick what kinds of risks they're taking?"

"What, you think you can tell a frog that by jumping into the water, he's still not safe from the rain?" Not expecting an answer, the head nurse walked away, his gurney squeaking between the beds, putting an end to silent prayers and perplexed expectations.

The most incredible thing to occur during this period, so favorable to somber thoughts, happened at noon on a Friday. The table was set as usual on the veranda. I'd taken a seat between Rover and Guzzler, alongside the other patients, whom I divided into two categories: the ones who'd accepted taking their medicine and sat down with us solely to escape their solitude as they waited for the sunset call to prayer by the *muezzins* who would authorize them to break their fast; and those, less numerous, who had found peace of mind in the concessions granted to followers who lack access to water to perform their ablutions (a stone suffices for purification), to pregnant or menstruating women, and even to the dying man unable to voice his profession of faith (a close relative or a neighbor witnessing this final hour can proclaim it in his stead). The latter group, armed with arguments that left an ashy aftertaste, ate resolutely and wildly, repeating to those listening that God, in his infinite mercy, never denies anyone from paying his debt at a later date, to which certain of the residents usually retorted: "And if you died right now with your mouth full?"

"Well in that case," the surly food-stand owner answered one time, "you can help yourself to my spot in paradise and set up a grocery store there while you're at it."

"You ought to be ashamed of yourself, blaspheming at your age!" said the teacher-lookalike, who was sitting apart from the others, buried in a magazine.

And Guzzler, between two mouthfuls: "You know, it's been a long time since I gave two shits about ending up in your camphor-filled paradise. I don't want to die of boredom amid schoolmasters and somber theologians."

"Well, the flames of Gehenna have been waiting for your kind for a long time too!"

"What do I care, as long as I'm hanging out with Brigitte Bardot and the stars of Hollywood!"

On the Friday I want to mention, nearly identical comments were being exchanged between those with mouthfuls of food and those without, in the perfect cordiality of dogs and cats, when a rock landed in the middle of our plates with a deafening crash. Women and young girls, transformed into harpies, gesticulated in our direction and spit out inaudible insults from the balconies and wide-open windows of the neighborhood buildings adjacent to the hospital wall; next to them, kids, delighted at their good luck, amused themselves by throwing stones at us, their joy exploding in a thunderous clamor when they hit their target. The rocks knocked over chairs, spilled plates, and shattered water glasses, and forks and spoons fell to the ground. After this altercation, we decided to move the table inside. Several windowpanes were smashed to bits and, despite taking shelter inside the hospital, we could still hear them shouting insults. It was impossible for me to get used to this world's angry and defeated face.

RAMADAN CAME TO a close at the end of a labyrinthine dream and the days returned to an unremitting sameness. In the dream, I was relentlessly haunted by the idea that the dead don't exist except within us. After running for so long, a glowing fire burned in my lungs and my legs could no longer support me. Thousands of insects fluttered through my night like seagulls, which only I was able to hear. But this time, the insects were visible, I could even feel them in my hair, hopping on tiny clawed feet. Stretched out among clumps of weeds, amid the smell of open graves, I knew that I was in a cemetery, which didn't bother me at all. I tried to control my breathing, inhaling air through my nostrils and exhaling through my mouth, quietly, at calculated intervals; but the biggest surprise, in this dream, was that I was able to recognize the different butterflies that my naked body attracted like a light: Urania, Vanessa, Bombyx, Argus, Machaon, and Phalene specimens, countless teeming larva, and caterpillars, in a nasty swarm. "This muck has been feeding on our rot," said the old man, my companion from the bastards' resurrection. I don't know how I recognized him since his face was covered in pieces of rank flesh. He knelt down in front of me with a kettle full of water and casually began performing his ablutions, not at all bothered by the maggots raining down around him as a result of his deliberate movements. He continued, "Goodness, Ramadan almost got me this year." Hysterical laughter rose in my throat, followed by a cough that nearly strangled me. "Are you making fun of me, you little beggar?"

"No, not at all," I responded. "So you're saying Ramadan follows us through eternity?"

"What eternity?" sighed the old man.

When I got to the end of the dream, it was almost dark outside. Behind the broken windowpanes, the fading light wavered between a faded pink and the sepia of an ancient photograph. A strange and inexplicable force drove me away from my bed. I went out into the cold. Rover, seated on a bench not far from Wing C, legs tucked under his chin, wasn't moving. His pajamas were soaked in dew. It's not possible, I must still be dreaming. Rover looked up as I got closer. "No, you're not dreaming. Not anymore. I'm not part of your dreams." I understood even less. How had he heard what I was thinking? And what was he talking about anyway? What a harebrained idea, that he wasn't a part of my dreams, as if it were possible to enter and exit someone else's dream. It was definitely Rover talking to me, but in an exceptionally serious and solemn tone. Most people, faced with situations that are beyond them, will react in their own way: they'll light a cigarette to gather their composure, or burst into laughter, or perhaps close their eyes, or, better yet, run away. But I found nothing more comforting than pissing at the base of the nearest tree. Rover kept on talking behind me: "I lied to you the other day, I don't know why actually. Maybe it's true, what that bastard Guzzler always says, that lying's become my second nature."

I turned around: "What did you lie to me about? Your mother? I had my suspicions, you know."

"What I told you is from at least two years ago. My mother

had 'really' died and the hospital administration gave me permission to go to the funeral. I was terribly afraid that day, afraid of taking the bus and attending the burial, and one of the most absurd thoughts got stuck in my head, which seemed unshakably logical at the time: if ever I was dumb enough to rush to the house, my mother's death would become definitive the second I laid eyes on her body. So, on that day, without knowing how – I must have looked like a sleepwalker or a crazed junkie – I found myself in a dark movie theater (impossible to know which one it was now); despite my state, I recognized Jerry Lewis on the screen; he was talking to a doll, speaking so tenderly and so sadly that time eventually evaporated. As if by magic, my pain disappeared, the people around me had left too, and in the silence of the roar of projectors or fans, I was no longer conscious of the distance separating me from the screen – there could no longer be any distance since I was 'on' the screen next to Jerry Lewis; he was talking to me and I was crying even though I was only a rag doll with long rabbit ears and bear paws ... Everything I told you after that is true, including the moment that I spit on the old creep." He stopped talking. I didn't say anything. I sniffled. I was so confused that instead of screaming to wake myself up under the warmth of my blankets, my hand grabbed a pack of cigarettes from my pajama pocket; I shook it so that one came out, and then handed it to Rover. When you're dreaming in spite of yourself, knowing there's no point in losing your patience when time has no meaning, and that it's not unpleasant to drift along, you quickly discover the principle of slow motion. In the moment between grabbing a cigarette from the pack and lighting it, a locomotive whistled in the distance, a dog barked and, as the crowing of a flock of roosters pierced a dawn growing bigger millimeter by millimeter, our reality – the anodyne reality of two friends smoking cigarettes, sitting next to each other on a hospital bench – took on the consistency of the curls of smoke escaping from our lips. I had to clear my throat twice before I could make an audible sound. I barely recognized my voice, which was saying: "If what you told me the other day actually happened two years ago, where were you during the twenty-four hours you were gone?"

"Nowhere."

I resigned myself to waiting for the rest of the story. After a few minutes, during which I thought that Rover had dozed off, he continued. "Do you remember the big iron gate that you walked through the day you arrived?"

"Of course."

"Have you seen it since?"

"Uh ..." (I felt a sort of emptiness in the pit of my stomach).

"Have you tried to find it again?"

And there it was. The dream was subtly sliding into the sinkhole of my nightmares, and for a fraction of a second I heard Guzzler laughing: "Hey, Smart-Ass has lost his marbles!" I stood up abruptly. "What's all this about anyway? What's your point?" Rover stood up as well and, his eyes locked on mine, said: "Just this: I've been looking for that damn gate for years so I can get the hell out of here but I have yet to find it again!"

SOMETHING GAVE WAY in the monotony of the days – or else in me, I don't know anymore – and yet nothing appears to have changed, everything continues, same as that first day, to the rhythm of a clock out of time, calling out the seconds, weeks, months, with ceaseless diligence. After living on top of one another, confined within four walls, acquiring practically the same movements, the same behaviors, the men are now all the same age; their laughter rings clear, with disarming nonchalance, their gazes settle indifferently on a wild flower in bloom for twenty-four hours, a dead rat, an autumn crocus, a falcon that's escaped from a fairytale, or a season apart from all the known seasons. Nothing surprises them. Childhood and old age burn in their eyes in a single bonfire. As for their memories – they're not much different than a dog's. When I went back to my bed at dawn, leaving Rover in the park, alone, in the middle of his absurd nightmare. I didn't turn around. I slipped under my clammy sheets, my heart racing, and slept like a log. I remember a time when I abandoned a friend in the same way, on a deserted street, under the wan glow of a street lamp, without turning around to see if he had left or if he was watching me leave; I slipped under my blankets in the small bed of a cruel child, slept for thirty years, and when I woke up, I went outside, convinced I'd find my friend under the same streetlamp. He was my only friend, but I no longer re-member his name or his facial features or the sound of his voice. I don't even remember why we were friends. I've told myself hundreds of times that he's surely dead by now, dead like everyone else I abandoned in the limbo of the past to run away, alone, toward the future. Well shit. All this forward movement, across tomorrows, kilometers, weariness, hope, sadness, celebrations, to end up in a future surrounded by high walls! One day, I learned that my friend was alive, that he was my age – that you're still alive and that you're my age. You chose to live like a troglodyte. I heard that you shut yourself up in your bedroom, in the dark, and haven't moved since, like a plant or a mineral. Behind your curtains, death chases the reckless and foolhardy, marking them, and you, crouching, hear children outside playing with a ball, you hear them aging … I can't imagine you surrounded by dreams, by ghosts, completely rigid, resolute, gulping in great breaths of sweet madness. But what do I know? Nothing could be more ordinary than learning about the death of someone's father, that a bad driver ran him over like a greenfly or that he was shot with a 7.65mm bullet in the back of the neck or in the gut, that he'll no longer walk in the front door, that he'll no longer kiss you on the cheek while he hands you cash to go to the movies. And so what? He's dead, goddammit! What would you have me do, slash my wrists, kill somebody, set fire to something, damn it all to hell, just because your dad breathed his last? You understand that death, anyone's death, doesn't make a difference in the grand scheme of things, right? Good. You hole up in your little shack, grow your hair and fingernails like an idiot hermit who worships eels and sacred fish, you gorge yourself in the shadows, you crap in a chamber pot, you breathe in the stubborn stench of your own shit, you make pets of your lice, bed bugs, crabs, the rats and cockroaches procreating under your bed, and what is it that you want to prove to the world? The world doesn't care, but your mother does. She tells you: "You need to get married, son!" You growl like a puppy, and demand some hot tea and cigarettes. Since I wasn't brave enough to visit you in your rat hole – you can't visit the past with impunity, you leave your blood and sweat behind, you leave it all behind, and it's rare to emerge from a mass grave in one piece – I imagined you in a scene from a movie, in black and white. All that I can make out in the darkness are your cracked walls, your rotting ceiling, your faceless head marinating like a rock lobster; I sit on the mat in front of you, I say hello, you say nothing, I ask you how you are, you say nothing, I could have chanted the sixty verses of the Quran and you would have said nothing, well, no luck, I stand up, and here I am at the hospital, almost happy, light as an empty page. Now, leave me alone, okay? What's the point? The only way to get rid of your ugly face is to go vomit. Keep my photo as hostage. I'm off, and this time I'm really leaving, goodbye friend, goodbye Casablanca, goodbye my blue sky, my flowering streams, goodbye all my bullshit.

Strange as it may be, my faint resolve to endure begins to melt in the acid of boredom. I feel the break like a dying man abruptly woken, disappointed, trembling, in tears, who's just been told he will lead a diseased, short-lived existence, condemned to a phony immortality, the oblivious and pitiful fate of the premature fetus and the moth, the trajectory of the shooting star, the perpetual battle of the caltrop. From now on, I'll get drunk, blacked-out, I'll quietly take my barbiturate every day, I won't pull on my leash, my breed being poodles and cowards, I'll kindly take care of my childhood paraplegia (I promise!) and loyally and patiently like my brother the camel – with no hard feelings – willingly like the donkey and mule of fables, adorned in a mantle of baseness and devotion, I'll recite the prayer book of the Hemiptera at every sunrise, I'll respect (I swear!) the slightest comma and even the haphazard punctuation of flyspecks.

LIGHT THE COLOR of incurable sadness filters through the room's broken windowpanes. I sit at Rover's bedside. I can barely hear him breathing, his head's under the pillow.

"You asleep?"

"Yes."

"And you're answering me?"

"Yes."

"Get up."

"No."

"It's sunny outside."

"Here too."

"Under the pillow?"

"Yes."

"Are you mad at me?"

"Why?"

"Let's go see our friends."

"I'm tired."

"Are you in pain?"

Rover removes his pillow, irritated. He leans against the wall. He doesn't look at me. He's so stubborn that not even the threat of death could make him yield. He extends the palm of his hand toward me, holding a crumpled plant.

"What is it?"

"Basil. It's the plant of the Prophet and sailors, it's an eye open to the future, the farmer's crystal ball. I had to walk in the park for a long time before I found some. Smell how good it is, like the blood of springtime, right? You just need to plant it in a little bit of dirt and water it, a few drops will keep it alive for a human eternity. I'm entrusting it to you, take care of it like it's your own flesh and blood. As long as it doesn't wither, I'll live, and if one day its green petals fade, well then ..."

"Well then I'll know not to count you among the living – my tears will flow until I'm very, very old! Are you done babbling, grandma?"

"I'm not asking you to believe me, just to obey me!" says Rover stubbornly.

"Why would I obey you?"

"You have to."

"Says who?"

"Try to fight yourself. Win or lose, you'll never know peace. I can see it in your eyes. Even if you want to convince yourself that you're a unique specimen, you don't believe it anymore than the rest of the nobodies do ..."

"What? Are you crazy, do you have bees buzzing around your brain, do you wash your hair once a year because you think you're the king of Persia?"

Smiling, Rover gets out of bed. He hands me the basil leaves and says: "Just take them and let's go have fun with the other madmen."

"DID YOU FALL on your head or something?"

"I'm not talking to you, half-pint. We understand each other, right Guzzler? A December without red wine is like Eid el Kebir without lamb. We all have to pitch in, boys!"

At the end of every year, the privilege of preparing and organizing the hospital festivities falls to Fartface. Nobody can say who exactly charged him with this task. But Fartface gets so energized by the process, exploding like a jack-in-the-box as he hands out roles and choreographs dance numbers, arranges jokes and sketches, that nobody would dream of challenging him for the responsibility, much less of trying to take over a single crumb of it. In any case, Fartface assumes command of operations in the first week of December. As soon as Rover and I arrive in his room, he pauses and, in his military voice, says: "Ah! I was just about to summon the two of you. Smart-Ass, you're my secretary and advisor, you're going to help me write my speech, it has to be good enough to make the most corrupt member of the Académie Française green with envy – you know, the guy who's used to plagiarizing old texts or hiring unemployed university ghostwriters. As for this clown ..."

"Don't count on me!" says Rover in a calm tone.

"We don't discuss orders. Especially today! I'm running out of time. Yesterday, a naive angel told me ..."

"Again?!" exclaims Guzzler. "If you keep contacting them, you'll get them all sick."

"It'd be funny to hear them coughing up in the clouds," O.K. chimes in.

"Shut the fuck up you morons, you pimply protozoa! This is really serious, fellows, I swear. 'He' promised to intervene on my behalf, so I need to prepare my funeral sermon!"

Everyone heckles him. Rover makes to leave the room.

Fartface grabs him. "Don't move, I'm not done with you yet, sweetheart."

"Back off, you old fool!"

Rover frees himself from Fartface's grip and quickly walks out. Fartface, speechless, turns gray. It's probably an effect of the ambient light.

"What's gotten into him?"

Fartface looks around. His gaze rests on me.

"What's gotten into him, huh?! This is the first time he's called me an old fool in that tone. Can you tell me what's wrong with him? Well, can you? The kid's never gotten angry before, he doesn't even know what it means!"

Fartface sinks into his bed, watching the group bicker. "You can't learn anything from hanging out with riffraff. From morning to night, it's nothing but brawls, insults, and profanities – a grand old time in short!" O.K. loudly declares, "I'm going to piss!" before leaving the room. "Monsieur is going to go pee, that's worth knowing, and what's more he announces it like someone saying 'I'm going to the U.N.' Hey, Guzzler, can't make the effort to talk correctly, huh, vary your vocabulary a little? Oh Lord, we must've arrived late when You dished out the assets to humanity! And the day when nothing was left but shares of politeness, courtesy, and kindness, well, we all must have been out sick!"

Seeing O.K. return, Guzzler sits up straight and cries out: "Son of a bitch! You didn't even go to the bathroom!"

O.K. lifts up one leg: "Warning!" And he noisily lets one rip.

Fartface sighs, concerned: "Old fool, me ..."

I look at him without saying a word. Suddenly everyone becomes serious. Guzzler, O.K., and the others stand up and form two lines. In the silence, Guzzler gestures to Fartface, inviting him to lead the "prayer." Cheerfulness restored, Fartface announces: "The imam's out of commission, make do without him, boys!"

Straight away Guzzler trumpets: "Dear Lord, Master of the seven planets and the seven heavens, have pity on our loyal corpses, send us a woman!"

"Allah, Allah!" chants the group.

"Just one adult woman will do!"

"Allah, Allah!"

"Even if she's obese, one-eyed, or has ringworm!"

"Allah, Allah!"

"Let's not get carried away," murmurs O.K.

"Silence in the ranks! Let's pray brothers, let's all pray, our popularity is on a radical decline in the slums of paradise! We, the begetters of chaos, we the brothel-born children of discontentment and complaint, we the eaters of ryegrass, nettles, stink bugs, and wind, we the eternally satisfied, dying, burping, blessing, giving thanks, may the seven saints pull some strings for us the day the scores are settled to get us the supreme aperitif! Sidi bel Abbas es-Sebti, Sidi ben Sliman, Sidi Abd el-Aziz, Sidi el-Ghezouani!"

"Et cetera, et cetera!"

"And Sidna Souliman ben Daoud who splashes in the seven waves of the Apocalypse, and Laqraâ Bensensens, and Sidi Zeblaz the virile!"

"Et cetera, et cetera!"

"And Sidi Bouâtoutou and Sidi Kaouki and Sidi Wassay and Lalla Rahma and our two-horned friend Alexander, and Cheddad Bnou Ad and Napoleon Bonaparte, and all the lay-abouts, the overindulgers, the narcs, the degenerates, the slave drivers, the pukers, the pen pushers, the masturbators, and in alphabetical order, those present, Bou-Rass the ambi-dextrous, Chewing Gum, Fli-Fla, Nesma, Windshield Wiper, and the rest of us, masterpieces made of foreskins and pros-tates, let's humbly bow down, to the ground, noses in per-fumed shit, and say ..."

"Amen, amen!"

THE SECOND-TO-LAST NIGHT falls hard, my head's eating away at me, scattering me to the four winds. I cross over into a section of infinity, surrounded on all sides by pending files, moldy paperwork, and shelves overflowing with x-rays of lungs. Rover is eying me, speaking words that I can't hear, one of us is breathing from inside a jar, no doubt about it, now he's yelling in French, in English, what are you saying? New York, Mexico City, popcorn, hamburger-frites, what are you talking about? Slow down, for fuck's sake, can't you see we're almost to Paris? Last stop, everybody off! "Argan's dying." Speak clearly, dammit! All I can hear are waves breaking, and somewhere there's a damn door slamming, slamming, slam! What time is it? Leave me alone, go rot in your sleep, there's people around at night, huh? What do they want from me? I haven't finished my chapter on Fartface yet ... "Argan's going to die ..." he thinks he's the Emperor of China, what does he expect, that I'm going to go on and on about his whole life story? What did you say? Since birth he's been wiping his ass with newspapers, as good a way as any to educate yourself! What did you say? "Argan ..." Shit and shit, I'm thrust into the cold, my dream leaves at a gallop, and Rover's still here, shaking my rib cage, okay, okay, I'm here, what is it?

"Argan's going to die."

"What?"

"He's breathing in and out like a leaky bladder, he's not going to hang on much longer."

"If this is a joke ..."

"Come on, he's in his bed, he's been throwing up rivers of blood nonstop, he's going to take the big leap soon and no wall is gonna hold him back."

Argan looks at us with startled eyes, he clenches his fists, forces out a smile – he's sweating profusely. Fartface puts a hand on his face, comforting him: "Hang in there, you're not going to desert us now, are you?" He talks to him about Christmas presents, paper lanterns, cakes, and candies. "I can't see you guys anymore." Argan sits up like an injured animal: "I'm seeing funny!" I can't take it anymore, I walk away from the group, I'm shivering, it's as cold as the North Pole. Guzzler is sitting outside on a step, he tries to pull himself together, hiccups loudly, sniffs, swats at the air around him, telling Rover to "let it go," but Rover persists, insists: "You yourself said that none of us will ever get better, remember, or are all your memories locked away, too?"

"Leave me alone!" sobs Guzzler.

I intervene: "Leave him alone!"

"Get lost, Smart-Ass, go finish your shitty chapter."

Guzzler lifts his head, two moons reflected in his damp eyes: "You too, Rover, get lost, my friend is dying, and you're telling me I should leave. Go, go, go, but go where, goddammit?"

"Someplace where the sun is up, where hope isn't dead, where there are flowers!"

"You know where you can put your hope, and your flowers on top of it?"

Rover does a kick, stumbles. "Bastard." He fidgets. "All you dirtbags are finished, you're beyond fucked!" He stumbles again in the dark, spits out some insults, moves under the trees; he laughs and laughs and keeps laughing until I can't make him out any longer. Then I hear Guzzler, moaning as he stands up – he wipes his eyes, the two moons are fixed on me. "You could have gone with him, you're the one who believes all that bullshit!" He turns around and enters the room in Wing A where death roams. I'm alone and I'm cold.

FARTFACE, THIRTY OR fifty years old, with a shaky memory, a vagrant wanted by the police of Heaven, arrested two
or three times, convicted and released for lack of evidence;
Guzzler, eighteen years old, notorious repeat offender; O.K.,
twenty-five years old, anti-Islamic intellectual; Argan, sixteen
years old, dead at dawn because he believes, like all the dead,
that dawn is the beginning of something; Rover, how can you
pin an age on that face? – reported missing, for good this time.
He also chose dawn to leave, but to where? – that's the real
question. North, south, east, west, the forest with its trees of
dubious genealogy, its silent rivers draining dirty bandages,
red and yellow cotton balls, and empty vials, and a miserable
sun like a drop of light in our miserable lives. I'd like to imagine him one more time, for you, for me, picture that damn,
tireless jokester who, I hope, lost his way for once and for all.
Like an annoying fly, a dog that's too loyal, he keeps coming
to the rescue, I see him advancing, and the more he advances
the more the night widens and multiplies, the more the trees
grow disproportionately around his small chromosomal frame
while, in all directions, the past, the present, and the future,
blind and dumb meteors fight their way through the leaves.
He's wearing an old backpack filled with pride, misdeeds,
clowns laughing or sobbing in their melodramas, phony love
stories, and mirrors, filthy surfaces reflecting tangled alley-
ways, forking, fading, or petering out in the mud. There are

no sidewalks, sewage drains, or electricity; my old roads run alongside wheezing, humid houses that are governed by the generous laws of the heavenly stick, of the father lost amid the warmth of women, and by the no less generous laws of God's blessed poverty, trickling out, through his merciful will, redemption by credit or cash or receivable over a thousand years of fasting. The brave jokester leaves, with my hagiographic sky haunted by disparate ancestral hordes stinking of mothballs, henna, and urine, penises and swords drawn, prancing on their horses into swamps of glory, and interminable and pathetic vanities. Now he's disappeared completely around a bend in the path; he'll continue to march toward a charitable sunrise, hoping to finally find some old-fashioned hospitality on his route, caravans of tribes tirelessly fleeing to protect the manuscripts of the Maghreb. I know he'll continue to walk, at each sunrise he'll be twenty years old, with a cargo of memories that he'll scatter along forbidden roads, in vain, because the cornered and scattered human race to which he belongs unlearns, on every day offered by its god, the game of living memories, the eagle's flight into a dazzling sky replaced by the falcon's terrible and blind descent. Now, he's disappeared completely, carrying a large part of me along with him. The little that's left of my atrophied, sick body makes do with its new solitude, surrounded by my sad characters in a celebration laden with pitfalls, joyful as an interrupted laugh. I don't know by what coincidence I find myself in the large television room, among dark coats, heads squeezed into towels or bare, escaped from a Brueghelian delirium; a strange serenity comes over me, it makes me think that a new edition of the bastards' resurrection is possible, that it's not only possible but horribly ordinary since it's governed by the inhumane law that everything perpetually repeat itself. The only difference is the much wanted fluctuating and ghostly margin between an imposed reality and a dream, a dream of seductive cruelty desired by the unhappy soul seeking release amid unnatural horrors. I stay seated within this margin, under a pallid light. At my side are the evening's four volunteers, dressed up as women: Guzzler, with his blond wig, looks like a ceiling broom; O.K., who's outrageously made up thanks to a burnt wine cork and scarlet lipstick, is playing the prostitute on her way home; the other two, Chewing-Gum and Windshield Wiper, mouths pursed, bicker like two true gossips, delighted to have spotted a shadow in the neighbor's window. The antics are gathering steam. Once they've gotten rid of a burly fellow obsessed with the idea of marriage, the four women have to contend with the advances of one guy that looks like a beanpole and another chubby-cheeked kid. The game would have gone on endlessly, in utter frenzy, if Fartface hadn't gotten up behind the makeshift podium. His low voice forces the dying racket to retreat. He begins to talk in a monotone voice, completely deadpan, like someone who's learned an old text by heart and is in a hurry to get to the climax. After a while, something unbelievable takes place. Reality is being distorted, it's impossible to explain with mere words. As Fartface drones on to the audience, prompting laughter interspersed with noisy coughs, another Fartface, more physically present and more intimate, is talking to me, directly, and not the slightest word of this private monologue is noticed by anyone else in the room. It's only later that I truly become aware of this strange anomaly. In the moment, I listen attentively and receptively, like a well-behaved child receiving fatherly advice, without the slightest bit of surprise, so perfectly still and relaxed that you might take me for an eccentric used to seeing people splitting in half since the beginning of time, forewarned that astonishment and shock would be inappropriate reactions.

This is what Fartface tells me: "It's undoubtedly not too late for me to make up my mind, for a second or so. I think you've understood for a while now that the idea of duration is entirely unpredictable here. I don't mean to say that time doesn't exist, that it flows through people on the outside, aging them a little more each second. It's probably even more present within these high walls surrounding us, so dense and cramped that we can touch it. That's what's so terrible. We have the ability to touch time the way you'd touch a consenting thigh. But despite that calculated, automated repetition, day and night, under the sun and moon, we're possessed by the horrible certitude that the same day, and the same night, are alternating with all the fidelity of a nightmare. I mean, yes – of course! – a flood of small details emerges to make us believe that something's changed, details so necessary that I'm absolutely certain we would all be mad without them. We've been in this hospital – let's call it that since, in a way, we are being treated here – for years. I can't count the days because their deceptive number has in fact been reduced to a single day that lasts 'inside' of each of us, and that day is a single point that can contain the entire universe, infinity. For all intents and purposes, it's pretty much like the word that, according to the theologians, encompasses God, a word that is of course impossible to find, and that an eternity wouldn't suffice to discover. Everyone who's come here – and you're one of many – has confused that permanence with boredom. In your somewhat special case, your faculty for dreaming and imagining has shielded you from error. You've lived among us without ever really being with us. Your moments, brilliant and fleeting, have tossed you around like a shipwrecked sailor, from one shore to another, from memory to hallucination. But you shouldn't believe that the patients here consciously know what they're experiencing. No one's aware of even the tiniest morsel of truth. And if I bothered to tell them, to expose the terrible mechanism governing this hospital universe, well there's no doubt about it, nobody would swallow such an absurdity. So I carefully restrain myself. Their hell is already unbearable, living as they are in the expectation of imminent death, waiting that becomes all the more abominable because it takes place amid total inertia. For them, every day that goes by proves their uselessness in life and at the same time rein-forces their hope for a better, more merciful tomorrow. So what would be the point in taking away that glimmer, even if it is superfluous? I sense the countless questions jostling in your head. I can't answer many of them for the simple reason that I don't know. For the rest, you'll figure them out yourself, you have enough time, seeing as you've decided to stay here. Incidentally it's that decision – which I don't understand, but again I'm not here to understand – that prompted me to talk to you like I never have before and never will again. Now that you're free, I don't want to know how your good sense will guide you. It's also possible that your memory will refuse to retain all this. And in that case . . ."

I NO LONGER remember the exact moment that I stood up and left the room.

A few stars sparkle in a pale sky. Far away, on a country road, shrill car horns fill the silence, undoubtedly partygoers roaming the night to express a transitory joy. It's this humid air, I think, that echoes the slightest noise across space. Seeing as it's going to rain soon, I hurry to get back to my bed. I can hardly see anything as I walk, taking care not to veer off the winding path bordered by tall grass. On my right, Wing A, with its lights off, looms between oak trees that quiver in a breath of wind. I immediately reject the dumb thought that Argan will appear at the entrance. The incredible thing about this hospital is that people never mention the dead – as soon as a lifeless body gets taken to the morgue, no one seems to worry about it anymore. I have yet to overhear a conversation praising the dead, the way you normally would. Apart from Rover – with whom I had a discussion about the old man (in a past that I'm now certain wasn't real) – I never had the courage to approach anyone and ask about the departed. Truthfully, the fear of confronting my own obvious amnesia always stopped me from satisfying my curiosity. I eventually convinced myself that I am no different from those long-ago voyagers who landed on islands on the fringes of the known world; their curiosity dulled quickly when faced with the impenetrable customs of a people hastily judged at first glance to be primitive and savage. Thankfully the superfluous and quasi-absurd pretension that I am surrounded by animalistic humans has evaporated, leaving behind nothing but a bitter humility, full of confusion and silence.

When I reach the structure of low, fortified walls that everyone refers to as "the morgue," I don't know what compels me to hurry, even more than I did while circling Wing A. All of a sudden, I stop, feeling so ridiculous that I look around me, worried I'm being watched by someone who won't hesitate to make fun of me. I make out the fleeting glow of a cigarette near the three steps leading to the hallway to Wing C. Nonchalantly, I approach the figure sitting in the cold night. I detect what sounds like a short mocking laugh. The moon, cleared from behind a trail of passing clouds, faintly illuminates the man's face. I recognize the tall skeleton who, according to Rover, forced his wife and her lover the barber to continue having sex while he watched.

"It's funny to see there's still someone afraid of dead bodies."

"I'm not afraid of dead bodies. I'm just cold. Why aren't you in the main room? They're having lots of fun inside."

The man scowls. His weariness makes him seem vulnerable to me. I climb the three steps and then turn toward him.

"Why didn't you have the courage to kill them? A normal man would have made short work of them."

His response surprises me: "But I kill them every night. I'm actually starting to get tired of it."

He abruptly turns sideways. A small metallic sound reaches me in the silence, like an iron object sliding and falling onto hard ground. The man bends over to pick it up. He's holding a finely sharpened axe between his two hands.

"I just chopped them up into pieces again."

"I don't see any blood on the axe."

"Why would there be?"

I stop listening. I enter the wing, feel my way to my bed. The storm erupts. I light a cigarette, I smoke it slowly. From time to time, I flick ashes in the darkness around me. I hear the rain. Fat, warm drops, like the rain that sometimes falls between summer and winter, during autumn, which, for us, passes very quickly. I lean against the wall and close my eyes. A blinding flash of lighting suddenly illuminates the doorframe, neatly revealing the silhouette of the man armed with his axe. I feel him watching me, the gaze of an ordinary man who hacked his wife and her lover to pieces. He takes a few steps in my direction, staggering like a drunk. He stops at the foot of my bed.

"You're not afraid?" he asks me.

"Of what? There's never any blood on your axe."

"That's true."

Very quickly he leaves the room. I open my eyes. Nobody's there. The rain is forming a sparkling curtain in the doorway. I slide under my blanket, thinking that sleep will consume itself like a burning piece of paper. When there's nothing but ashes left, I'll once again wake up in the light of a new day and walk behind the veranda, to the spot where I planted basil leaves at the base of the wall.

For now I'll sleep. It makes me smile to think that I imagined a murderer brandishing his axe. Something to scare a child, just a sick child sitting by the fire. Since I'm no longer that child, and I can never be him again, I decide to stop writing. For that matter I have nothing else to say.

1987–1989

Translator's afterword

BEFORE MAKING ITS way into English, *The Hospital* was translated into Arabic by the Moroccan writer and journalist Mohammed El Khadiri, whose challenge was to render a text heavy with colloquialisms and slang into modern standard Arabic (MSA), a formal and mostly written version of a language with dozens of regional variations. English may be more accommodating of informal speech than literary Arabic – and indeed welcoming to any number of *isms* (neolog-, regional-, colloquial-) – but nonetheless, for me, translating the dialectal language of Bouanani's novella demanded particular care and creativity.

For example, the ubiquitous French conversation starter "*Ça va?*" "*Ça va.*" typifies the difficulty in translating Bouanani's dialogue. Literally, the expression means "It goes?" "It goes." In other words: "How's it going?" "Good." Or: "Okay?" "Okay." A contemporary equivalent: "Hey, what's up?" "Nothing." Or the even more succinct: "Sup?" "Nothin." The magic – and frustration – of this phatic expression is that it can be and is used in the French-speaking world in just about any situation: a salutation between two prisoners, two neighbors, two new friends, two old friends – there is no equivalent English expression with as much flexibility and nuance.

On page 102, Bouanani uses the expression to convey the

monotony of the hospital setting, as well as the resigned familiarity that develops between its residents. The register here is simultaneously informal and formulaic; the interlocutors respect an understood order and rhythm of speech, and a crescendoing verbal one-upmanship. They "excel at the art of talking without saying anything."

Dialogue also allows Bouanani to show off his talent as a cineast with an attentive ear for timing and theatricality. My challenge was to find equivalents for the coarse, acerbic, and sometimes sophomoric speech that Bouanani uses to reveal the social differences among the hospital patients, without caricaturing any of them.

I took care to avoid the pitfall of inadvertently modernizing the text with contemporary slang (e.g., translating "*Ça va?*" as "What's up?") or creating a forced informality by hewing too closely to the source text. (In the Arabic version, El Khadiri chose to translate this section of the text, as well as other dialogues, into Darija, or Moroccan Arabic.) This type of challenge was compounded by the importance of conveying that Bouanani's novella is a resolutely Moroccan text, written in standard French but interspersed with regional words and expressions.

In *The Hospital*, the landscape of Morocco – its trees, plants, fruits, and animals – stand in for a vanishing precolonial culture, and naming this highly specific landscape in translation demanded research into terminology and etymology. No mere fly caught in a web, but a dipteran doomed by its stupidity; palmipeds whirling through the sky readying for attack; unbridled manchineel and calabash trees.

The taxonomy of flora and fauna, smells and tastes, saints and legends permeates *The Hospital*. With amnesia as the disease, and time itself in question, Bouanani delights in naming things – weeping willows and cyclamen flowers, prickly pears and esparto grass, Sidi bel Abbas and the two-horned Alexander – to anchor his characters' memories and dream lives.

Yet Bouanani's characters remain largely anonymous – "rumpled blue pajama[s] among other rumpled blue pajamas" – distinguished only by the monikers assigned them by a similarly anonymous narrator. These adventurers and fools and derelicts represent the invisible heirs of Morocco's fading past; their names assume a great importance, a way for the narrator to identify and reclaim these individuals, marginalized and worse, forgotten, first by a colonial regime and later a bureaucratic and oppressive new state. I attempted to replicate both the meaning and sonority of those nicknames in my translation: "Guzzler" to evoke the youthful bravado of *Le Litron*, slang for a cheap liter bottle of red wine; "Rover" for the wanderer *Le Corsaire*, his French name synonymous with adventure and sea voyages; and "Fartface" for *Le Pet*, the old clown with a juvenile nickname.

These men – for the hospital is an overwhelmingly masculine domain – tell their stories for many reasons: to pass time, to impress or intimidate, to remember. They tell their stories with longing or bitterness, mirth or pride. In Bouanani's original text, this male cacophony of voices is accentuated by his attention to poeticism, rhythm, and humor; his style is a blend of dense, page-long hallucinatory ramblings through memories and dreams (and perhaps hell) and dialogic scenes characterized by irreverence, irony, and nonchalant violence.

Immersion was key to my approach to translating this many-layered novel: immersion in the history and culture underlying the story and immersion in the language. To grasp the cultural context of the novel required research into the social inequities prevalent in Morocco during the 1980s; the folklore of coastal villages near Rabat and Casablanca; historical references spanning Moor-ruled Andalusia to World War II. Immersing myself in Bouanani's language was more instinctive – with each translated term or expression, I asked myself: How does this word sound? Is this phrase too literal or artificial? Does it flow? Do the raunchiest parts make me laugh? And, for the novel's final passage, do I have goose bumps, as occurs each time I read Bouanani's ending in the original French?

My goal was to render a difficult text accessible to new readers, while remaining faithful to Bouanani's mission: to resuscitate a fading culture and bring its members, men without bearings, without names even, to life in "black and white." The stories shared by the absurd brotherhood in Wing C may be depraved, grotesque, or farcical, but they are as uniquely important as the odes to Moroccan mythology, animals, plants, song, and food that intersperse the text. The stories reflect the author's fascination with personal and collective memory, and their overlap with history. Little wonder that *The Hospital* is awash with second-hand stories recounted by gossips and liars, and a constant calling into question of their accounts.

Throughout the novella, the reader is forced to wonder: What is real? Who among the hospital's madmen can be believed? What truly happened and what didn't? Can the narrator himself be trusted? In the end, the fatalistic storyteller concludes that it doesn't really matter. But regardless of veracity, what Bouanani's characters say – and how they say it – does.

– LARA VERGNAUD

Acknowledgments

Lara Vergnaud would like to thank Diane Bensenia, Tynan Kogane, Chris Clarke, Heidi Denman, and Mohammed El Khadiri for their insight and feedback, and Omar Berrada for his continued support and encouragement.

Anna Della Subin would like to thank Touda Bouanani, Omar Berrada, and Ali Essafi for sharing stories of Ahmed; Emma Ramadan, Joshua Richeson, and Robyn Creswell for their translations; the editors of *Nejma* and *Souffles-Anfas: A Critical Anthology*; Susan Gilson Miller for her history of Morocco, and Leor Halevi for his scholarship on the angels of death.